STAR

STRUCK

TRANSITION

RI'CHARD J. CALDWELL

Back cover photo taken by Prestige Portraits
www.prestigeportraits.com

ISBN: 978-0-578-05360-8

Published by MoMas Press

Printed in the United States of America

STAR STRUCK
TRANSITION

For my Mom, thanks for believing in my dreams. Always. To Phillip Smith, thanks for not getting mad about my late night writing. To Taylor Sage, thanks for the "inspiration". And all my friends in San Antonio, Mesquite, and Denton. Couldn't have done it without you all.

Contents

Warning

Be sure to read "The Prologue" before you start chapter 12. If
you skip the prologue, you will not understand the story.

Thank you.

The Prologue

The cargo hold of the plane was the first to go. Its doors were rattling uncontrollably then they flew off the hinges.

The fuel tank ruptured next; spilling gasoline like rain to the land below. The left wing's turbine engines exploded suddenly, sending the aircraft plummeting from the sky. The pilot and co-pilot were dead and the passengers onboard were screaming, crying and hyperventilating. The oxygen masks dropped down from the compartments but everyone was too panicked to utilize them.

A handful of hysterical passengers wedged the fuselage door open and jumped out, hoping to die of a heart attack before they hit the ground. It was pure chaos onboard and I couldn't focus. My friend Kyle and I waded through the madness to cockpit. Neither of us knew how to land a plane but we had to try something.

Autopilot was disabled and there were too many buttons to B.S. our way through. The plane's altimeter showed that we were dropping hundreds of feet per second. It was hopeless; we were going to crash.

"Why, Kyle?" I asked my friend. "Why did you do it? You've doomed us all, you realize that, right?"

"I'm sorry, Franklin. I lost control." He replied.

The right wing was ripped from the plane and we entered a downward freefall. Kyle and I were snatched from the cockpit, pulled to the back of the plane and pinned to the wall. The passengers were frozen with fear because they knew what was coming. And as they all prayed for their lives to be spared, I began longing for simpler times. Like a few months ago when I was standing at my front doorstep, on my birthday, with a gun to my head and my father as the wielder of the weapon. Ah. Those were the days…

Chapter 12

"Explanation"

Explanation: To make clear; to give the reason for.

Um, ok. So, this was officially the worst family reunion ever. I couldn't speak. I stumbled backwards and fell in terror at the sight of the firearm. I wanted to run but my body was too uncoordinated.

"Can I come in?" My dad asked then entered without my permission. The smoke detector blared loudly as soon as he set foot in the door, or, at least I thought it was the smoke detector. Was this a security alarm that I didn't know about? The noise came from the doorpost. A flashing light that resembled a police siren emerged from a hidden compartment in the ceiling. *That has gotta be new*, I thought.

My dad was all business. "I know you're confused," He screamed over the alarm, "But I'm doing this to protect you!"

Oh yes. Holding your only son up at gunpoint is sure to win you 'Father of the year', I thought.

My dad steadied his hand and pulled the trigger. The bullet exploded from the barrel and spiraled rapidly towards my frontal lobe but, as it grew closer, the projectile began to lose momentum and then it stopped moving; in mid air. The alarm overhead ceased spinning and the ringing was silenced. The world around me was frozen. Time was standing still; I was the only thing moving. *Am I doing this?*, I wondered.

Before I had time to gather myself up, a tall woman, approximately 5'9 or 5'10 with light brown skin and dark brown eyes, appeared. She wore a dark blue suit that was formal yet

1

feminine and it fit her lean figure well. The woman had high, sculpted cheekbones and soft, almond shaped eyes. When her eyes met mine, she smiled and as she did so, she revealed a small gap between her front two teeth. I knew this woman well.

"Mommy!" I cried when I recognized her.

"Thank goodness you're alright! I thought I would be too late!" She replied cheerfully.

Ok. Now I was seriously confused. I looked at my dad, who was still suspended in animation (gun in hand), and I looked back at my mom.

"What's going on?!" I yelled.

"First of all, *who* do you think you're talking to with that tone of voice? And second, I'll explain later. We must go. When you get up, watch out for the bullet; if you touch it, it *will* unfreeze and you *will* be shot." She said.

Good to know, I thought.

With that in mind, I inched past the bullet, which was milliseconds away from splattering my brain on the wall, and joined my mom.

"Where are we going?" I asked.

"Don't worry about it. You're with me. So, relax and enjoy the ride." My mom replied.

I know she meant for that to be comforting, but, considering the morning I was having, my mom's statement made me uneasy.

Without warning, my mother and I vanished into thin air and, moments later, everything at my house resumed its normal speed. The bullet continued its path and burrowed straight through the wall. When my father realized that I was gone, he knew just who was to blame.

"Elizabeth!" He seethed, calling my mom by her first name. Irate, my dad stormed out of the house, slamming the door on his way out and, as he left, the siren finally stopped wailing.

*****

Explanation

Limbo was nothing like what Derrick had imagined. Derrick found himself in an empty room with navy colored walls. The room was bright but there was no light source to be seen.

"Hello?" He called and his voice echoed off of the walls. "Hello?!" He yelled a bit louder.

"Who are you talking to?" A voice answered from nowhere. Derrick spun around swiftly to find the origin of the sound.

Whoever this is, he's from Chorifier because that Seoreh he's speaking, Derrick thought.

"That is correct, Sivart." The voice replied to Derrick's thoughts.

"Who are you?" Derrick asked, in Seoreh as well.

"I'm you." The voice answered. The voice was coming from behind Derrick.

He turned around and saw…himself, a younger version. The younger Derrick was in human form. He couldn't have been older than 13. Derrick was taken back by the physical manifestation of his past. The illusion had bright red hair with dark green eyes, stood at about 5'8 and was staring at Derrick, unblinking. His hair was on the longish side, almost completely covering his eyes. He had an average body type, slightly more tone than average.

"What happened to us?" Young Derrick asked.

"Why are you here?" Derrick asked.

"Wow. Answer my question with another question. Nice." The younger one retorted. "Why have you changed? You weren't always this evil. Heck, you weren't evil at all. What happened?"

Derrick didn't have a reason. "I don't have time for this." He muttered. How do I get out of here?"

"You don't. You're trapped inside your own mind and the only way out is to face you inner demons." The young Derrick told him.

The older Derrick was getting impatient. "You're going to show me the way out!" Derrick said in a strange voice that sounded like his normal voice layered with another, deeper voice. He was using his *hypotique* ability.

"You're wasting your energy. Powers don't work here. You can't sweet talk your way out of this. For the first time in your life, you'll have to deal with your problems."

Derrick sighed. *I'm never getting out of here*, He thought.

*****

The Phalanx hadn't lost hope yet. Ever since Chris went AWOL, Sarita, Danny, and Hannah have been searching for him. They filed a missing person's report a few weeks after he disappeared but it yielded no results. The three friends were starting to get discouraged. They met at Ladent's, a popular joint down the street from Lincoln high.

Ladent's was very teen-oriented. The inside was dimly lit and filled with video games, pool tables and Air hockey tables. There were tables to eat on scattered throughout the restaurant. Orders could be placed at the concession stand near the front door and a waiter would bring you your food and a few complimentary tokens to play games after you're done eating. In a booth near the front door sat a teenage girl, no taller than 5'3, with caramel skin and jet black braids that stretched down her back. She wore glasses with thick lenses that made her dark brown eyes look larger than they actually were. She was joined by a slightly taller, olive skinned guy. He had bluish green eyes, dark brown, shaggy hair. He had a slightly athletic build and a scar over his right eyebrow. The guy was carrying a cheeseburger and fries on his tray. It was Sarita and Danny. They were waiting on Hannah to arrive.

"He just doesn't want to be found, dude." Danny said in between bites of his greasy cheeseburger. "Usually, people who run away *don't* want to you to find them."

Sarita cringed at the sight of Danny chomping down on his burger and grabbed a French fry from his plate before he could protest.

"That's not always true," Sarita argued, "Sometimes people run away as a form of crying for help."

"He killed his girlfriend. He needs time to deal with that. When he wants our help, he'll come back."

"What if he never comes back? What will we do then?"

"There's nothing we can do." Danny said then sipped his soda.

Sarita ate her stolen fry. "But his family thinks he's dead! They're worried sick. And we can't tell them what really happened because they'll think we're crazy." She paused and then continued. "I just feel so guilty. And what about the Tsol Battle Championship? We can't compete without 5 members."

Danny had forgotten about that little detail.

He asked, "How are we supposed to compete without a group? Like, are we even a team anymore? Chris is M.I.A. and Xavier is a demented freak show."

He had a point.

As the two contemplated their next move, a Hispanic girl with very light brown eyes and hair, burst through the door. She was only 5'5 and she had an exceptionally lean figure. Her hair was up in two ponytails today. It was Hannah; panting and fatigued. Hannah lived three miles from Ladent's. She was checking her mail, before she joined her friends at the diner, when she found a letter, from Chris. Hannah read it and freaked out. She had to show her friends the note. They finally had a clue about Chris's location. Hannah ran the entire 3-mile distance to Ladent's on adrenaline alone. And she was very winded. Hannah slid into the booth with her friends. Sarita and Danny waited patiently for Hannah to catch her breath. It took her a minute to regain her composure.

"I got a letter from Chris." She finally said between gasps.

"What?!" Sarita and Danny screamed, causing entire restaurant to turn and stare at their table. "Um, sorry about that. Go back to your lunches." Danny called to everyone. "So, yeah. A letter? Would he really make it that easy to find him?" He asked Hannah.

"Well, no. There's no return address." She pulled out the letter to show her friends.

Sarita grabbed the envelope, unfolded the note and read it aloud.

Dear Hannah,

I need you and the others to stop looking for me. I want you all to know that I miss you guys terribly. I'm still not sure what to do next. I know Laura's death was an accident but I still feel partially responsible. So, for now, I just need to do some soul searching.

Sarita folded the note back into the envelope.

Danny looked satisfied. "See? He's fine and just needs time to think. Just like I said."

"How can you be sure he's fine?" Hannah asked.

"Well, he did write us a letter that said so and it's definitely his handwriting. What more do you want?" Danny asked back.

"I want Chris back and things to go back to normal." Hannah whispered.

While Danny and Hannah argued, Sarita was studying the letter and envelope for clues to Chris' whereabouts. The letter itself gave no answers, but the envelope was a bit more helpful. Hannah was telling the truth about the envelope having no return address but she failed to notice the postmark from when Chris sent the letter.

"Dude!" Sarita erupted suddenly, startling Danny, Hannah and the people in the booth behind them. "Look!" Sarita lifted the envelope and pointed to her discovery. The circular postal mark read: *Mailed from Hamilton, Bermuda.*

"Sarita, you're a genius." Danny said.

"Bermuda? How did Chris get to Bermuda?" Hannah wondered.

"Simple," Sarita answered, "The same way we're getting there-by plane."

"Finally," Danny said. "A game plan."

The three teens left a tip on their table and hurried out the front door of Ladent's.

*****

"You broke my heart, Curt." An illusion of Hannah whispered in Curt's ear. The illusion had been tormenting Curt for who knows how long but it was really getting under his skin. There was nowhere for Curt to hide. Curt was surrounded by full body mirrors, similar to the ones from the house of mirrors where he fought Hannah a few months back. He didn't realize it, but he, too, was trapped within his own mind.

It wasn't my fault. I couldn't control myself, He thought.

"Keep telling yourself that but it still doesn't heal the pain you caused!" Hannah's illusion accused. "Do your excuses keep me from crying myself to sleep at night? *No.* They don't." It continued.

Curt began to wonder if the real Hannah cried herself to sleep. He really missed her and was so guilt ridden by how he treated her while under Derrick's spell. Curt looked at himself in the mirror. His skin was still quite tan for an asian guy. He almost looked Mexican. His hazel eyes appeared to be strained. Curt's semi-long black hair laid flat instead of being up in its usual fauxhawk. Basically, he looked pitiful.

"She must think I'm a monster." He mumbled. "I'm sorry, Hannah. Will you ever forgive me?" He asked. The illusion of Hannah was caught off guard. "No, wait. Don't answer that. I don't deserve it. I should've been there to protect you but I was the one who hurt you the most. That is...unforgivable."

The once surly illusion of Hannah placed her hand on Curt's shoulder. "It's ok, Curt. She forgives you." It told him.

7

"She forgives me? Why are you referring to yourself in the third person?" Curt pondered.

"I'm merely an illusion; a test. You passed but you still have one more to accomplish. So, get going. Hannah's waiting for you." Hannah's illusion disappeared and a door formed in the distance. Curt sighed in relief that he had a chance to make things right with Hannah, and he intended to do just that. Curt entered the portal without hesitation; ready to face whatever task was at hand.

*****

Dr. Bronson was still searching, desperately for X. She had been looking for him for the past three months with no luck. She began her search when she discovered a prophecy that the world would end at the end of the Tsol Battle Championship and it involved X so she felt the need to seek him out, for the good of humanity.

She found hundreds of Xavier Gonzalez's around the world (none of which were any help and a few called the police on her.)

After successfully losing the cops, on her most recent attempt to find X, Dr. Bronson crossed off the Xavier Gonzalez in Austin. There was only one more Xavier on her list: Xavier Gonzalez in San Antonio.

If this isn't the right Xavier, the world is doomed, she thought.

It took Dr. Bronson a little over an hour to drive from Austin to the northeast side of San Antonio. She drove by Xavier's house but no one was home. She passed Lincoln High School but it was 5:00 p.m. so the school was vacant. Dr. Bronson even checked Lincoln Park. X wasn't there but she did find a homeless man who was ranting about Jesus not bringing him Christmas presents for St. Patrick's Day. She backed away slowly, hopped into her car and sped off.

Where is he? Finding one teenager shouldn't be this difficult, she thought.

Explanation

Dr. Bronson drove around aimlessly, searching for Xavier until she almost ran out of gas and had to stop at a local gas station to fill up her tank. As her tank filled up, Dr. Bronson planned her next move. She was so engrossed in thought that she didn't notice a forest green sedan pulled up to the pump behind her. A Hispanic teenager, with green eyes and short black hair stepped out of the driver's side. He was about 5 feet 7 inches tall.

"I'm surprised it's taken you three months to find me." The teen said, speaking to Dr. Bronson.

She turned around to see X filling his tank as well. "So, it's safe to assume that you're Xavier Gonzalez? I have questions." Dr. Bronson said.

X smirked. "Well, that's good because I have answers."

*****

The Staci I knew wouldn't have fallen for such an obvious trap. These words replayed over and over in Staci's mind. Derrick may have been in control of her mind but Staci was still conscious the entire time.

Sarita was right. I wouldn't have fallen for something so simple. Why did I? How could I have fallen for Derrick's trap in general? I was cocky, she thought.

Staci stared at her reflection on the marble floor she sat on, in shame. Her pale skin almost blended in with the floor but the black eyeliner she wore helped intensify the brightness of her brown eyes and they shined brightly on polished surface.

"Yeah. You really were." said an illusion of Sarita.

"Sarita?" Staci was puzzled. "You guys won. Why are you in Limbo?"

"I'm not. You're imagining me."

"Ah. I see. Awesome. I'm going crazy. But at least I'm not alone. Is this all I'm gonna do for the rest of eternity?"

"Only if you want to."

Staci was confused. "I have a choice?" she asked.

"Duh." Sarita's illusion mocked her bluntly. "You always have a choice."

9

Staci stood up, at 5'6, to tower over the illusion. "So, what are my options?"

The illusion laughed lightly. "Isn't it obvious?"

Staci shook her head.

Sarita sighed. "Well, you can stay here and rot away or you can fight."

Staci pretended to think it over then tied her hair back with the white scrunchee that she wore on her left wrist (which is an obvious sign that she meant business).

"Well, that's no choice at all. You *know* I'm a fighter." Staci said, confidently.

The two girls smiled at each other.

"Now, that's what I like to hear." The faux Sarita said. Behind her, an exit materialized unexpectedly. "Beyond that door is not the typical fight you're used to, so be careful."

Staci gripped the door handle and turned back to the illusion and said, "I always am." Then she opened the door and vanished on the other side of it.

*****

I had so many questions for my mom. No. Actually, I'm lying. I was brain dead. My dad had just tried to kill me then my mom froze time, teleported in from who knows where, and saved my life. (Best birthday gift ever, by the way.) All this information was too much for my mind to process at once.

Images blurred and whizzed by all around us as we traveled through space. Or were we moving through time? I didn't know, honestly. But it was all pretty cool looking. A rainbow of colors and shapes painted my vision and then it was over.

My mom and I appeared at Lincoln High School.

"What…what are we doing here?" I asked.

"There's no time to explain. I'll be back as soon as I can. Love you, Pork Chop." she leaned in to kiss me on the forehead then vanished.

Great, I thought. I sat on the pavement in front of the massive school.

Explanation

I didn't get the chance to ask her what her powers were, exactly or why she dropped me off at the school. Were there no other safe places to drop me off? Perhaps somewhere with food; I was suddenly starving. I guess near death experiences do that to you.

Lincoln High School was an eerily quiet place afterhours. It just towered over you, menacely silent; secretly judging your past actions in its halls. Ok, so, it probably wasn't judging anyone since it wasn't alive but what else was I supposed to do while sitting outside of my high school.

"Maybe I'll finally have time to sort out a few things." I reasoned. I stared into a puddle that was formed by a broken sprinkler head which sprayed uncontrollably hours earlier. My skin was pretty dark that day, but that's to be expected considering where I live. My dark brown, almost black eyes seemed to shimmer in the reflection of the puddle. Even in the reflection I looked too skinny for my age and the fact that I was 5'10 didn't help things. I ran my tongue over my teeth and then through the gap in my two front teeth. I knew it was wishful thinking but I had hoped that, one day, the gap would just disappear.

As I sat, pondering and staring at my reflection, I heard someone walking towards me from behind. They gave their position away when they stepped on a patch of gravel and the rocks scraped the ground.

It's way too late for a student to still be at school, I thought. So, as the stranger grew closer, I was charging a lightning bolt on the tips of my index and middle fingers. Whoever was behind me was in for a nasty surprise.

The steps were almost upon me when I whipped my body around and blasted the person with a surge of electricity. If I had waited a second, I would've noticed that the "mysterious stranger" was my dad.

The shot burned straight through his chest and exited from his back; dissipating as it traveled. My dad was speechless. He fell backwards and landed on the cement.

I walked over to check on him. The sidewalk could be seen through the hole in his chest.

I had just killed my father.

Oops.

*****

"You really don't have any powers to begin with." said Danny's illusion, accusingly.

"That's not true!" Jayden yelled. She had been taking the illusion's verbal abuse for long enough.

"Really? Oh. Right. You can copy abilities. How *cool*. What happens when no other super powered people are around and someone's holding a gun to your face?"

That was a good question. And every good question deserves an even better answer. "Have you forgotten who I am? I'm Jayden Annabelle Penaloza. I can do anything."

"Really? Anything?" the illusion asked.

Jayden was shocked that the illusion was standing up to her. This was a new experience for her. Jayden had brown everything: brown hair, brown eyes and brown skin. And, to put it simply, she was curvy (in a good way) so guys gave her a lot of attention. She had been referred to as a 5'4 bombshell and guys basically bowed down to her. With her brown hair, skin and eyes, she was always treated like royalty.

It was frustrating her to be treated like this.

"Yes, anything I set my mind to, I can do. Try me!"

The illusion of Danny smiled. "Ok." It said mischievously. A trap door opened below Jayden and she fell through it. "I hope you can walk the walk as well as you talk the talk." It called to her from above. As Jayden slid down the dark tunnel, she began to wonder what she had just gotten herself into.

*****

Oh no, oh no, I thought. *I'm a murderer. Do I call the cops? I mean, technically, he was declared dead years ago. Hmmm, what if I just walk away...*

Explanation

"Wow. That was not pleasant." said a familiar voice, interrupting my thoughts. When I looked back, my dad was sitting up. The fist-sized hole that I burned in his chest closed right before my eyes and soon, the only proof that he had ever been injured was the hole in his t-shirt. My jaw dropped.

"Carrie failed to mention that you now manipulate lightning as well. But I suppose I deserved that one seeing as how I tried to kill you earlier." he said, jokingly.

My mind was reeling. "I just killed you! How are you still alive?!"

My dad stood up and dusted himself off. "You sound disappointed. Aren't you happy to see your old man?"

I laughed out of nervousness.

"Honestly, I don't know how I feel about you right now." I replied flatly.

"That's understandable. I suppose I have a lot of explaining to do, and I'll tell you any and everything you need to know, but not here. Let's go home." he said.

It's not your home anymore, I thought but I followed him as he walked the twelve-mile distance back to the house (I wasn't sure why he didn't have a car but I figured it was best not to ask). I knew one thing for sure; I was going to need some serious therapy when this was all over.

*****

While I was walking home with my dad, an illusion of me was in Limbo, tormenting Jared. "You're a disgrace to all Pirate enthusiasts, you know that, right?" it asked Jared.

"I know! I know! I lost to a Ninja enthusiast. I'm so ashamed. I'm sorry!" Jared groveled pathetically.

"Why are you apologizing to me? I'm just the Ninja lover who beat you. Apologize to him." the illusion said and pointed to a lone Pirate appeared next to him.

"I'm sorry, Mr. Pirate, sir. How can I earn forgiveness?" he begged the Pirate illusion.

The pirate eyed Jared up and down. He was Mexican but you wouldn't be able to tell by looking at him. He had really light skin and dark brown eyes which could barely be seen since he squinted so much. The pirate thought that Jared could easily pass for asian, if his lips weren't so abnormally large. The pirate snapped his fingers and a ladder that led to an exit above revealed itself.

"You want forgiveness?" the pirate asked.

"More than anything." Jared said.

"Well then, redeem yourself. Climb the ladder that leads to your next test." Before the pirate finished his sentence, Jared had sprinted up the ladder and through the exit.

*****

Derrick and his Legion knew they were trapped in their respective minds, but they had no idea where their bodies were. While the teens were trying to escape their own minds, their bodies were suspended in fluid filled tubes. There were monitors attached to various parts of their bodies to keep track of their vital signs.

They weren't alone; there were many other tubes in the room. Most were empty, but a few had people in them. Behind Derrick's team, the elderly British woman's team could be seen, minus the British woman. She was nowhere to be found. My friends were in a laboratory of some sort. It looked like something straight out of a science fiction movie. All it was missing was a mad scientist to burst in and start experimenting on them.

In the laboratory, there were two people taking notes on the teens. The note takers were Hispanic, one male and the other female.

"Their brain waves have increased," The male said in a booming, deep voice. He was referring to Derrick and the Legion. The male stood at about 6'1 and was pretty buff. He wasn't huge but he could easily break me in half. He had light brown, kind eyes and a gentle smile. His hair was gelled down and he wore an off-white lab coat that made him look older; even though he couldn't have been older than 16. "I don't know what to make of it." he continued. "What do you think, Delilah?"

The female, or Delilah as the guy called her, thought about it then said, "Er, I dunno, John. If I had to guess, I'd say they just passed the first test." Delilah was almost the complete opposite of John. She was very slim and was only 5'7 with straight black hair. They had their eyes in common. Hers were light brown and made her look like a gentle person as well. They were clearly brother and sister; Delilah being the older one by two years.

"I think we should tell the boss about our findings." John suggested. Delilah nodded and the two opened the front door and left. As it closed, a label could be seen towards the top of the door. It read: Limited Interaction and Maintaining Basic Observation. Spelling out the acronyms: L.I.M.B.O.

Chapter 13

"Clarification"

Clarification: To make or become clear.

"Where are we going? No, never mind. I remember where. But why? Why should I even go with you? You just tried to kill me! You and I aren't exactly friends right now." I said.

"Do you want to know how I'm still alive after you effectively scorched a hole in my abdomen?" he asked.

I'll admit, I was curious.

"Yes, I'd like to know that." I told him.

"I can regenerate and I can make others do the same. I was going to shoot you and then heal you a few minutes later. The people I work for really want you dead. I was protecting you." He said.

"Who do you work for?! I've almost been killed multiple times by people who wanted to find out who you work for!" I exclaimed.

"I'm sorry to hear that but I have something in my office that will explain everything."

After about an hour of walking, we reached my house. My dad's office is on the first floor, way in the back of the house. I waited at the office door while he rummaged through his old things. It was a weird feeling seeing him recklessly digging through his stuff like he used to. I hadn't let my mom throw out his stuff. Not yet. It had been too painful. She did remove all the furniture; leaving nothing but dusty boxes.

"Did you guys give up on cleaning? Your mother being the neat freak she is, I find it hard to believe that she just let this dust collect so badly in here." he said, elbow deep in junk and dust. Before I could respond, he had found what he was looking for. In his hands, he held a pair of overly futuristic sunglasses. They were bulky and had odd buttons and gadgets on them. There were obvious cracks on the lenses from the unnecessary pressure of boxes piled upon them. My dad brushed the glasses off.

"David sure knew how to build equipment back then. Still as sturdy as ever." My dad wore a soft smile on his face as he reminisced over days long gone.

"What are those?" I interrupted.

"My D-goggles. A friend of mine invented these for me so I could pass my story on to my offspring if I didn't survive to tell it."

I was puzzled. "What story?"

"My life during the TBC."

My eyes widened and a huge smile stretched across my face. "No effing way! You were in the Tsol Battle Championship?!"

"In it? I won it."

"Does mom know?!"

"I'd hope so. She was there when it happened."

"I do *not* believe you!" I was happier than I had been in the longest time.

"I figured you wouldn't believe me, which is why I dug up this fossil." He raised the D-goggles as he spoke. "It's much easier just to show you."

My dad handed me the goggles. "When you put the goggles on, you will relive the greatest moments of my life and a few that weren't so great but I don't wanna give anything away. You'll just have to see for yourself."

I put the D-goggles on. Nothing happened. "Are they broken?" I asked.

"No, they're just old. It'll take a second to warm-"

I didn't hear the rest of that sentence because the goggles activated. Everything went dark. It was deathly still and remained that way for a while until a voice asked: "Does it work?" It wasn't my dad's voice. There was a lot of bass in this guy's voice but I could still tell it belonged to a teenager; no older than 17.

"Um, I don't think so. I don't see anything." A voice answered the question. This was definitely my dad's voice; only it was higher pitched as if he were in the transition period between puberty and adulthood.

"You're not supposed to see anything yet. It's empty. The Diary goggles need to have memories in them first." The teen took the goggles off my dad's face and he could see again. The teenager in front of my father was clearly Ecuadorian by all the trinkets he wore. He had very light, olive toned skin and had on thin glasses that he probably only wore to look smart. The teen was about 5'9 and was surprisingly buff considering he was obviously a nerd. His hair was gelled up into a fauxhawk. He had on a black t-shirt that had the Ecuadorian flag on it and blue jeans.

Who was this guy? I thought.

"Diary goggles? David, you're my best friend but that is *the* worst name you've ever come up with. Ever. How about D-goggles?" My dad suggested.

"The name doesn't matter, man. It's the fact that these goggles are the future of history books." He pointed at the D-goggles for emphasis. "A video diary that can record for 20 years straight before it runs out of space is revolutionary."

My dad stood from the foldable metal chair he was sitting on and flicked the rim of David's glasses. "You're ahead of your time, bud. Light years ahead." David smirked.

The two friends were in a poorly lit basement, possibly David's parent's basement. There were tables along the walls covered in test tubes, filled with various chemicals and wires and many other technical, half-finished gadgets.

"So, are you ready for this Tallest Beagle-" My dad started.

"Tsol Battle Championship." David corrected him.

18

"Yeah. That. Can 'Leahcim' really be trusted? I mean, we just met him a few weeks ago. It was your science experiment that gave us these...abilities. We don't have to do this. We can just as easily walk away from this all."

David wasn't persuaded. "Aren't you curious about aliens? I think it deserves a shot."

My dad sighed. "Ugh. Alright. Let's go find Eliza." he said.

"Oh, you mean your girlfriend?"

My dad punched David in the chest. "Shut up and let's go."

The video got really fuzzy and I heard a lot of static. The screen went white. When the image appeared again, three years had been skipped; probably because of the damaged lenses. My dad, David, their friend Eliza, and two other people were gathered around a purple gorilla with the head, neck, and tail of a coral snake. *Dude, it was King of Chorifier!* I thought. *Was he in the TBC too? This is nuts.*

"I thank you, my human friends. This TBC victory wouldn't have been possible without you all. I will remember each and every one of you. As Prince of Chorifier, I can promise you that, as long as you don't tell any other humans about the TBC, you will retain your abilities." The five teens nodded

"If you ever need anything, you know where to find us." My dad offered.

"I will remember that for future reference." The Prince said, then teleported away. David and the other two went their separate ways, leaving my dad and Eliza alone.

"Eliza..." he said, grabbing her by the hand. "We've been through a lot of danger situations these past few years..."

"Yeah?" she asked, expectantly.

"Well, it's got me thinking about a few things." *Dude, I think he's about to propose*, I thought. "I almost lost you a few times during this tournament and each time was harder than the last and now that the TBC is over," My dad fumbled around in his pocket, pulled out a ring box, and dropped to one knee. "I never want to lose you again."

He opened the box to reveal an engagement ring. "Elizabeth, will you marry me?" Eliza's eyes began to well up then tears flowed freely.

"Yes! Yes! I will marry you!" She exclaimed and my dad took the ring, slid it on her left ring finger, and they hugged for a while. Eliza interrupted the special moment with an excited but awkward statement, "Elizabeth Rae Stanton has a better ring to it than Elizabeth Rae Lamberg but I'm old fashioned so Lamberg it is." They kissed and, as they did, the picture began to fade out again. Just in time. I did *not* want to see my parents making out.

The goggles skipped six more years, past the wedding, to a few weeks after my birth. There was a pearl white crib in a pink room.

"I'm still mad that he wasn't a girl." My mom muttered. "We painted the room for a girl. How did this happen? We should sue the doctor, that's what I think." My mom and dad were watching over me as I slept.

"It doesn't matter. We have a beautiful baby boy. We should be happy." He told her although he was secretly happy that I wasn't a girl.

"Happy? How am I supposed to be happy when my son's name is Fiona Elizabeth Lamberg?!" My mom was a bit irate at this point. Whoa. What? My name was Fiona? *Not* cool.

"We'll just get his name changed." My dad offered, optimistically.

"To what?" She snapped back.

"Franklin Isaiah Lamberg."

"No." My mom said flatly. "He can have your middle name as his first name but he can't have two of your names."

"Then what will we name him?"

"Franklin Josiah Lamberg."

My dad was speechless. "Josiah? Why?"

My mom grinned. "Because it's not Isaiah."

The sound crackled and became static as the memory disappeared. The D-goggles fast-forwarded another year, my first birthday. My mom and I were on a towel on the living room floor of our old house. She was pretending to eat my feet and I was laughing hysterically.

"Mommy's little man is turning one today!" She squeaked in a baby voice. "Yes, he is! Yes, he is!" I had no idea what she was saying but I was enjoying it. I was wearing a red one piece footie pajama outfit with yellow lightning bolts on the chest and my mom was wearing a pair of basketball shorts and a shirt from her high school track days.

A knock at the door disturbed the game we were playing. My dad, who had been sitting on the couch, answered the knocking. On the other side of the door was a vicious looking gorilla with violet fur and the head, tail and neck of a snake. My dad frowned, seized the creature firmly by its arm and pulled it inside our home.

"What are you doing?! Where's your hologram? People can see you! Leachcim! Are you listening?"

The gorilla hybrid shook his head. "My father died."

My dad's expression faded. "Oh. I'm sorry."

"Don't be. Before he passed, he said I was next in line for the throne. I'm the new King of Chorifier."

"Oh. Congratulations!"

"Thank you. This brings me to why I'm visiting: I would be honored if you, Eliza, and David would be my royal advisors."

My mom looked up from me to lock eyes with the future King of Chorifier. "Are you serious? We would love to. How do we start?"

My dad and King Leahcim looked at her with surprised expressions on their faces. She had answered pretty fast, giving it no thought at all. The baby version of me began to giggle and I uttered an odd word. It sounded bubbly and incoherent but I repeated it until someone understood.

"Plasx," I tried.

My mom whipped around to face me. "What did you say?" She asked, eyes wide.

"Phlosx," I tried again.

"What are you trying to say, sweetie? Phloox?"

"Phalanx!" I said a final time and laughed.

Wow. I didn't remember that. Strange.

The picture disappeared again and all I could hear was white noise. Five years passed and the video returned. I guess I was six years old by now. My dad almost had a full beard. Five years of working for the King of Chorifier seemed to have reaped many financial benefits for our family. We had moved out of our old, one story house and into the two story that we live in today. We had two new cars and my parents seemed happier than ever. Many TBCs had come and gone since my parents competed and none had entered again since, though they still stayed informed on what happened during them. Actually, that was their job. The King of Chorifier only asked that my dad and his friends monitor the contest for any irregularities because, in 10 years, his sons would follow in his footsteps and enter the TBC; the King wanted them to have every possible advantage available. The adults agreed to this task and they'd been watching the tournament for the last five years.

My mom and dad's shift had ended an hour ago and they were at home, helping me with my homework.

"Ok. Wait." I said in a mildly highly pitched voice. "5 + 5 is 10 and 3 + 7 is 10 *and* 4 +6 is 10 too?" Math frustrated me when I was that age.

"Yes," My mom said with a nurturing tone. "2 + 8 is 10 as well."

"And so is 1 + 9." My dad added.

The six-year-old version of me frowned and asked, "Am I old enough to drop out of school yet?" My mom and dad laughed even though I was dead serious.

We were about to move on to a different problem when the house phone rang. It was David.

"Hey, David," My dad said when the phone was up to his ear.

"We've got a problem, Isaiah." David said. It was David's turn to monitor the TBC so my dad already knew what it was about. Something happened in the TBC.

"How big of a problem?" He asked, lowering his voice so that my mom and I couldn't hear.

"That depends on how fast we act. A small resistance group, who call themselves the Defense Against Nefarious and Seemingly Hostile Aliens, or D.A.N.S.H.A. for short, is growing larger. Not only that, they have started to sabotage the contestants of the Tsol Battle Championship. Most recently, they've kidnapped a contestant and stole their medallions. Luckily, D.A.N.S.H.A. wasn't in the TBC so stealing the medallions meant nothing and they just dissolved into sand and returned to the King. But D.A.N.S.H.A. will be back. I'm sure of it. I have a feeling that they're looking for a way to enter the TBC."

My dad tensed up a little and cursed under his breath. "What does King Leahcim have to say about this?"

"He wants you and Eliza to investigate. Find out what you can."

My dad shook his head. "No. Eliza stays here and takes care of little Frankie. I'll go alone."

David sighed into the receiver. "Fine. I'll tell the King. But be careful. D.A.N.S.H.A. is becoming a force to be reckoned with." David hung up the phone and my dad did the same. He rubbed his eyes with the thumb and pointer finger of his left hand.

My mom looked at my dad when he rejoined us. They made eye contact and immediately she knew what was going on. She stood up, hugged him tightly, kissed him on the cheek and said, "Whatever you have to do, just come back in one piece."

The picture went out just as my dad walked out the front door. Nothing else happened for about two minutes and all I could see was darkness. The memories soon returned and when they did, the first thing I saw was my mom and dad arguing.

"You're doing work on our anniversary?!" My mom exploded.

"What do you want me to say? I've been investigating D.A.N.S.H.A. for five years now and I have *nothing!* Going undercover is my only option." My dad responded.

"After 16 years of marriage, you didn't think that I'd be a little upset that you took us on a cruise liner, for our anniversary, just so you could fake your own death?!" My mom was on the verge of tears. It was heartbreaking to watch. My dad pulled a jewelry box out of his pocket and took a gold necklace that had a soaring eagle charm on it. He placed it around my mom's neck and fastened it.

"Happy Anniversary, Baby." he whispered in her ear. My mom held her composure until he left the room, but as soon as the door shut behind him, tears streamed down her face and she grasped the eagle charm between her thumb and pointer finger.

Outside the room, my dad walked to the rail of the ship, waited for a rough patch of water, then "fell" overboard.

The D-goggles shut off after he hit the water and I took them off.

"Well?" My dad asked when I came back to reality.

"I see you in somewhat of a different light now. So, what happened after you jumped ship?"

My dad thought about it a little. "Well, I swam ashore and after a few tests of loyalty, I was initiated into D.A.N.S.H.A. The process took a few years to accomplish but it was worth it. Well, at least it was at first. Until *you* entered the TBC." We sat down on the floor of my dad's old office and he continued his story.

"D.A.N.S.H.A. found a way to enter me in the TBC and I was assigned to watch Prince Drahc'ir and Sivart and when I heard that Prince Sivart lost, I reported back to D.A.N.S.H.A. HQ. They were pleased that one of King Leahcim's sons had lost but they weren't completely satisfied. They wanted both aliens out of the way. The two were considered to be a major threat to D.A.N.S.H.A.'s plan. I was against this because killing Drahc'ir would result in killing you. And, although they didn't know that you were my son, they sensed my hesitation."

I was shocked. "What did they say?" I asked, nervously.

"They said it would be my final test of loyalty. They said they had been having doubts about where my allegiance lied. So I agreed to the task."

"It took three months," he continued, "to come up with a plan. But then it hit me: I'd shoot you then heal you a little while later."

I was speechless. I had no idea what to say but my dad didn't pause long enough for me to think of something. "D.A.N.S.H.A. has spies everywhere. I'm sure they know that I didn't kill you by now so I need to leave and find a way to ensure they don't come after you to finish the job."

"Uh...alright." I said, dumbly. "Wait!" I called as he touched the front door knob. "If you can heal, what can mom do?"

My dad smiled. "I'm sure she'll be back soon. Why don't you ask her?"

*****

"Whoa. Whoa. Explain it to me again." Xavier was having a hard time grasping what Dr. Bronson was saying. The two were sitting on the hood of Dr. Bronson's hybrid car. She was trying to simplify the prophecy so that X could understand.

"Ok. Well, if some group named D.A.N.S.H.A. wins the 'Tsol Battle Championship', they'll use one of their rule free wishes to grant everyone in the world powers but it will back fire on them, millions of meteors will crash into the earth, killing billions of people and making the planet almost unsuitable to sustain life."

"Ah," X said. "I see. That's sobering news." In all honesty, Xavier didn't foresee this. Actually, his powers had been on the fritz since the Phalanx broke up. Many things had been going wrong for X since the team split up. And now that impending doom was looming around the corner, he knew he couldn't do this alone.

"Ok, Dr. Bronson, you've come to the right place. If we act fast, we can save the world and keep that horrible prophecy from occurring. But…I'm gonna need some fire power."

Chapter 14

"Reconciliation"

Reconciliation: To cause to be friendly or harmonious again.

I've never had good luck. I never won contests, games, or the lottery (not that I'm old enough to play, but I doubt I'd win if I was). My mom and dad have superpowers, and they're on opposing sides. I really don't know who to trust.

I tried to de-stress by watching TV. Nothing was on. Birthdays shouldn't be this stressful. It was a Friday. The weekend was coming. I'd have a few measly days off then back to school. But I didn't wanna go. I didn't want to do anything anymore. I felt betrayed by the people I trusted the most. My mom and dad kept these huge secrets from me. X and Derrick didn't value my friendship as much as their stupid TBC. This was ridiculous. I needed some air. I grabbed my house keys, walked out the door, and started jogging; still in my pajamas. My appearance was the least of my concerns.

A few minutes after I had left the house, X and Dr. Bronson were at my doorstep. They knocked a few times, no answer.

"Now what do we do?" Dr. Bronson asked curiously.

"I have a spare key." X said nonchalantly.

Man, in hindsight, I probably should've taken my spare key back.

He fumbled through his pockets until he found a bronze key. He inserted the key and the mechanism in the door unlocked. X peered inside and knew right away that the house was vacant.

"We're running out of time!" Dr. Bronson insisted.

"I know. I know. Just give me a s-" X grew silent, midsentence. His pupils disappeared and his eyes were solid white. He was having a vision. This was a first for Xavier. He had always had his visions as he slept; never in the daytime.

A worried Dr. Bronson screamed his name but X was nonresponsive. He was in his own world now. In this vision, Xavier saw me, standing in line at the DMV, waiting to take the picture for my driver's license. The line was ridiculously long. It would take hours for me to reach the front. In the vision, time lapsed and suddenly, I was next in line. The elderly woman behind the counter urged me to stand behind the yellow tape. I kindly obliged. I stood as straight as I could.

"Smile real big." She said in a feeble voice and she took the photo. The camera's flash was so bright that I didn't notice the bullet that blasted from the camera's lens. Before I could even react, I had been shot, right between the eyes. The impact launched me into the wall and I slid to the ground; leaving a streak of blood on the wall as I went. Chaos broke out at the DMV after I had been murdered. Then the vision ended.

"Xavier?" Dr. Bronson whispered.

X looked badly shaken. "We have to get to the DMV. Now!"

I walked and walked until I couldn't go any further. Oddly enough, I ended up at Lincoln Park. I hadn't been there in ages or at least it felt that long.

I plopped down onto the weed-infested lawn and just laid there. It was quiet, but not creepy quiet. The sky was cloudless. There were no birds. No planes. The sky was empty.

I'm not ashamed to admit that I wanted to cry. I wanted to disappear. Nothing was what it once was. My old life was stolen from me. *This isn't fair!* I thought. But then again, life never is…

My pocket began to vibrate. I didn't notice at first but the caller was persistent. I snapped out of my trance and checked my phone. It was X. I hadn't talked to him since…the incident with Laura. What could he possibly want? And, more importantly, did I want to talk to him? I pressed *reject* and the call went straight to voicemail.

I needed some trivial task to take my mind off of things. I thought about it and remembered that today was still my birthday. My 16th birthday. And as such, I was supposed to get my driver's license picture taken. I hopped up, dusted off the stray blades of grass and headed to the DMV, oblivious to the danger that awaited me there.

"Hey, You've reached Frankie's phone. Obviously I'm busy *or* ignoring you. Either way, leave me a message and I might listen to it." X hung up on the voicemail message before the beep sounded. He sighed. X was in the passenger seat of Dr. Bronson's car. They were headed to the closest DMV; it was only a block away from Lincoln Park.

"We have to hurry. There isn't much time." he told her.

Dr. Bronson nodded and slammed down on the accelerator.

I was so excited to get my license…until I saw the line. It was enormous. I had never been to the DMV and if the lines were always this long, I decided I would never be back. The line stretched outside the brick covered building.

"This is so lame." I muttered.

"I couldn't agree with you more." said familiar voice from behind me.

I was afraid to look because I knew who it was.

"Come on, Franklin. You gotta talk to me. I'm sorry, O.K.?"

I wasn't budging. Not a word.

"Please?" he begged, but I was content with giving him the cold shoulder.

X preceded to spend the next few hours begging for my forgiveness, the line grew shorter in the process.

"What is it going to take for you to forgive me?" X begged.

"Look, X, what you did was unforgivable. It's going to take some life-altering situation for us to be cool again. Now, if you'll excuse me, I'm up next." I walked up and the elderly woman behind the counter told me to stand behind a yellow line of tape that was on the ground and I did so.

"Smile real big." she said.

"No!" X screamed and tackled me as the picture flashed. The bullet narrowly missed my head. We hit the ground hard but we were both still alive. I looked at the hole in the wall left by the bullet then looked at X. The woman who had been behind the counter had suddenly vanished without a trace.

I smiled at X, embarrassed. "Alright...we're cool."

"So, what do we do now, David?" my mom asked. She was on her cell phone as she walked down the aisle of a local grocery store. She was pretending to be shopping as a cover.

"He's with Xavier now. He'll be fine for the time being. I'm sure this is all overwhelming. Give him a few weeks. At the most, three months." David answered.

"I hope you're right." My mom hung up the phone, grabbed a random item, and headed to the checkout counter.

****

Three months had passed since my 2nd assassination attempt and things had been relatively quiet. I had time to relax and sort things out. X filled me in on everything: The prophecy, Dr. Bronson and all things in between. We had discussed it and agreed to get the team back together if we had any hope of winning the TBC. And I knew the first place to start.

Danny was working out at *23/6*, the gym that was about eight or so blocks north of my house. It was a hot spot among teens but the gym was dead. It was a Sunday evening at 8 p.m.

during Christmas break and the gym was dead. He felt this was the perfect place to "practice". There were no cameras and no witnesses.

Danny changed into a lime green tree frog and bounced around on the exercise equipment. He leaped from the stationery bike and did a front flip in midair. As gravity began to kick in, he morphed again; this time into a grizzly bear. He smashed into the ground with a loud thud.

"This was a bad idea." Danny stated. He was too big to maneuver around the room with all the machines crowding the space.

"Good job," X said as he entered the room.

Danny hopped to his feet and growled ferociously. X backed up.

"What are you doing here, dude?" Danny asked and stood on his hind legs to look more menacing.

"Relax, Danny. He's with me." I said as I stepped in between the two.

Danny returned to his human form when he saw me, revealing that he still wore the orange jumpsuit that my dad gave him. "Bro, you're cool with Xavier again? What's going on?!"

I sighed lightly. "It's a long story. But suffice to say he's a good guy."

Danny looked at X, then back at me. "Whatever you say, Flames."

Hannah and Sarita were in Sarita's room, trying to figure out how they would get to Bermuda with only 200 bucks between them. There was a world map spread across Sarita's bed. Hamilton, Bermuda was highlighted on the map and the quickest route was displayed by a dotted line going from San Antonio to Hamilton. Chris' letter was on top of the map.

"Flying is totally *not* an option," said Sarita, discouraged. "Unless Danny turned into some kind of giant bird and we flew on his back…but that kind of strain could kill him."

"We could always driv..." Hannah's voice trailed off before she finished her sentence. She was going to suggest driving but, ever if they had a car, driving would only get them to Florida.

"Did you miss us?" Danny exclaimed as he burst through Sarita's door, Xavier and I close behind.

"Not really. We saw you yesterday." Sarita said, bluntly. Her eyes wandered passed Danny and locked onto X. Hannah did the same.

"What's *he* doing here?" both girls asked coldly.

"It's all good," Danny explained. "Xavier's cool now. We're getting the team back together."

"Yes," X added. "Now, all we need to do is find Chris."

Hannah, Sarita, and Danny met each other's gazes when Xavier's said Chris' name. There was an unspoken agreement between them: No one tells X about the letter. Although I had forgiven X, my friends had not. Hannah slyly hid Chris' letter under her leg and Sarita covered the map destination with her palm.

"What are you guys working on?" I asked.
A guilty look appeared on the girls' faces. They didn't want to lie to me but couldn't tell me the truth with X around. Sarita put on a fake smile and said, "Oh, nothing. Just homework."

Chapter 15

"Deception"

Deception: To cause to believe an untruth; to use or practice

deceit.

My mom chose the one day I had time to just relax to show up again; bringing lots of excitement and even more drama. It was December but it was 60 degrees outside. I loved the San Antonio weather. I was lying on the roof watching the birds fly by. I didn't have anything planned that day.

The shingles were scratching my exposed arms. I was only wearing jeans and an orange shirt that said, "You Wish" in green letter. I was thinking about how relaxed I was when she popped up out of nowhere.

"Hey, Pork Chop." she said nonchalantly. Her arrival startled me and I slid off the roof; grabbing the rain gutter at the last moment. The gutter buckled as my weight pulled down on it. Two bolts popped off as the gutter gave way. I was screwed. I wouldn't die from the fall but I'd surely break something.

"A little help!" I called as the rain gutter said a final farewell and detached from the house. My mom selflessly leaped from the roof, caught me and teleported us to safety just as the gutter clanked on the sidewalk below.

"Mom," I said as we traveled through space and/or time. "You need to wear a bell or something so I know when you're coming."

"I'm sorry, hon. I just had to get to you before your father came back."

This statement confused me.

"Why? Dad's a good guy."

My mom had a look of disbelief on her face. "Is *that* what he told you? Let me guess. He showed you his diary goggles. And I'm sure he failed to mention the parts he erased."

Erased? I thought. *That would explain the static.*

"What did he erase?" I asked, afraid of the answer.

"It's true that he went undercover to get secrets on D.A.N.S.H.A.," she said, "but he soon earned a position of power within their ranks and he became power hungry. Not long after, he started giving away Chorifian secrets and many other horrible things that pushed me into the arms of his best friend, David."

She offered to show me her D-goggles as proof but I declined. I could see the look in her eyes. It was the look of a truly hurt woman. My mom wasn't lying about this.

"So, what do you need me to do?" I asked solemnly. I was still a bit in shock that my own father had become a villain.

"First, we go see David." And just like that, we arrived. I didn't know where we were but wherever it was, that's where we were. Wait. Scratch that 'cause it made no sense. But wherever we were, it was very cold and bright. The walls and floors were made of stainless steel. We were standing in a long corridor. Everything was so polished and shiny, I was kinda afraid to walk on it. I was sure I'd scratch it.

There were onyx colored doors on both sides of the hall, positioned a few dozen feet apart. As we walked, I read the signs. Most were just one word-*Maintenance, Boiler, Equipment*. Pretty normal stuff.

As we continued down the never-ending hallway, I saw a door that stood out from the rest. It read: *Limited Interaction and Maintaining Basic Observations*. None of the other doors had been as detailed as this one. I couldn't explain it but I was strangely drawn to this room. I had to look inside. I grabbed the doorknob. It was cold to the touch. I began to turn the handle but before I could open the door, my mom placed her hand on my shoulder.

"You're not ready to see what's in there. Not yet." she said. Instead of arguing like I normally would, I listlessly obeyed.

We continued down the hallway for about a minute or two more then it opened up into a vast, sphere shaped room. The floor turned into a suspended bridge that connected the hall to a large circular platform. It was surrounded by ridiculously high tech equipment but, if this was the same David from my dad's D-goggles, I'd expect nothing but the best technology everywhere.

And it really was the same David. He may have been twenty years older, but he still looked the same, still wore Ecuadorian gear, and still had the same glasses that made him look smart. He was working on some equipment when we first saw him. Sparks were flying everywhere and whatever it was that he was doing probably required safety goggles; which he was not wearing.

"Shouldn't you be wearing goggles or something?" I shouted as soon as we were within earshot.

He put down his tools. "Frankie!" he said. "Man, you're getting big. You're almost an adult now." He continued with a huge grin.

"You know, you really should be careful. We've gotta take care of that brain of yours." My mom added.

David seemed offended. "What about the rest of me?" he asked.

My mom shrugged in response and smiled.

The two adults hugged, shared a brief kiss, and turned their attention to me.

"To answer your question, Frankie, I've already calculated every potential direction the sparks could fly by factoring the angle of my tools, wind resistance and my distance from the sparks' origin."

Wow, he's smart. I thought. *He even makes me look dumb.*

At that moment, John and Dahlia walked in, followed by three others. There was a black girl with light brown skin, caramel colored eyes, and shoulder length black hair. She was 5'6, curvaceous build. She wore a devil red dress that seemed to conflict with the lab setting. She was gorgeous but I couldn't help but wonder where she was going, dressed up like that. Her name was Lauren Brown.

There was also a Hispanic girl with ridiculously thick glasses and oddly cut, short brown hair. She was 5'1 and had an awkward, yet genuine smile. She wore tight black jeans and a pink t-shirt with a bunny on it, saying something sarcastic and mildly hurtful. David introduced her as Janna Torres.

The last of the three was a guy. He said his name was Kyle Perez and he was much taller than the others; about 5'11. His skin was light brown but his eyes were dark. *Most likely Mexican*, I reasoned. He wore a shirt with the name of a college across the front (I had never heard of the school) and blue jeans.

"Frankie, I'd like you to meet a few friends of mine." David introduced me to Dahlia, John, Lauren, Janna, and Kyle then said something I never expected. "They all have abilities too."

*****

Danny, Sarita, and Hannah had done the math. Then they redid it. Over and over and over. And each time, they came up with the same answer-there was no way to get to Bermuda. Not legally, anyway.

"This is ridiculous. Why is it that we can manipulate nature, become invisible, and change shape but we can't do a simple thing like find a way to Bermuda?" Sarita was clearly frustrated.

"There *is* a way. We're all thinking it but no one else is willing to say it. We'll sneak onboard."

"That's illegal..." Hannah muttered.

"Do you have a better idea?" Danny asked.

"No."

"Well then. Let's go."

"Do you even have a plan?" Sarita asked, cynically.

"Don't I always?" Danny smiled widely and both Sarita and Hannah became very nervous.

*****

This was amazing! Outside of my friends from the Lincoln Park Meteor Shower, I didn't know anyone else that was like us. You know, *talented*. Now there were 5 complete strangers who could have any and every ability under the sun. The idea alone made me very excited; like a kid in a candy store. I had to know. After our initial meeting, I was given the opportunity to grill them for answers.

My mom and David went off to do...who knows what, leaving the five of us to chat. I had finally got my questions in order when Kyle beat me to the punch.

"What can you do?" he asked.

"Huh?" I was caught off guard.

"You're a full blood. There's no way you're powerless."

He was very blunt. I liked that. Kinda.

"Oh. I manipulate fire and lightning." I engulfed my left hand in white-hot flames and sparks bounced off of my right hand to demonstrate.

"Oh, you're cool." he said sarcastically.

I didn't like Kyle anymore.

"What can you do? Before you start judging me."

Kyle smirked. "I'm a jinx." he said slyly.

"Oh, you're tough."

"That's right. I control good and bad luck. I can do something good like make someone win the lottery or something bad like make a plane crash." His ability would soon come back to haunt me. I just didn't know it at the time.

My new friends led me to a room down the hall from the entrance. It was essentially a living room. The walls were bare and disgustingly bright yellow.

"I painted it," Lauren Brown said, proudly. "It's my favorite color."

I smiled politely as I stared in awe at the hot mess they called a room. The room was lined with burgundy leather couches. Janna took credit for the couch selections. I wasn't a fashionista or an interior designer but I was sure that taste this bad had to be illegal. There were no windows but the fluorescent lights overhead illuminated the poorly decorated room.

We all plopped down on a couch and the rest of the group took turns explaining their abilities.

"I can digest any type of matter: from a cheeseburger to a cinderblock." John explained, excitedly.

Delilah demonstrated her power, rather than tell me. She rose into the air, lifted by some unseen force and darted around the room; almost too fast to see with the naked eye.

"I can go intangible," Lauren said then phased her hand through the wall.

Janna smiled and said she had x-ray vision.

This was so cool. They all had such interesting powers. In someway, I was jealous of all of their powers. There was still something I needed to ask though.

"I've never seen you guys before. Were you visiting Lincoln Park on your own when you were infected? Or were you at the Amy Caster memorial pool?"

The five teens looked confused.

"Infected?" they parroted. "Infected with what?"

"Yeah, infected. You know. Mutated. Transformed. Changed. Where were you when you got your abilities and when did it happen?"

The teens had puzzled looks on their faces. *Am I not speaking English?* I thought. *Is there something on my face?*

"We've had our abilities for as long as we can remember." Lauren told me.

Ok. Now, I was the one who was confused. "What do you mean?" I felt so lost.

Kyle started laughing at me.

Deception

"Dude," he said, "We were all *born* with our abilities."

Chapter 16

"Progression"

Progression: To move toward a specific goal or further stage.

We had been competing in the TBC for about a year and a half now and we had really progressed as a team. And yet, we were worse than ever. Danny, Sarita and Hannah were keeping secrets, X seemed distant, and Chris was chilling in Bermuda.

My dad's team was fairing much better. Kinda. They were about to get their final two medallions but they weren't going about it in the traditional way: they were about to steal them.

It was 9:00 p.m. and pitch black outside. The only light source was coming from the street lights that cast a gentle glow on Brody, Timmy, Carrie, Rick, Alexis and my dad. They were all posted up behind a bush in front of a run-down mansion, similar to the Remington Estate (only this one hadn't been burned down by a certain shape shifting friend of mine). This mansion was a lot less complex than Remington was. This building was light gray and very wide. It was old but it looked like it could take a few more decades of wear and tear. The house stretched back for an acre or two. Obviously, the house had many rooms inside. There were about 20 guards protecting the front door, armed with all kinds of deadly weapons. The owner was clearly paranoid.

My dad glanced at his team. They were kind of a random grouping of teens. Brody was a very lanky kid with amber eyes who had often been described as a beanpole. He had a vanilla like skin tone and silver braces with blue rubber bands on them and a dorky smile to match.

Carrie was an equally skinny Caucasian girl standing at about 5'5. Her hair was light brown, almost dirty blonde with greenish brown eyes that had a calming effect when you stared directly into them and she just looked excited to be there.

Timmy was about 6'0 and his olive skind had a bronze-like gleam to it. His eyes were dark brown but whenever his light brown hair was in his face, his eyes appeared to be black. He wasn't really paying attention; instead he was drawing a smiley face in the dirt with a stick.

Rick Lorette stood at about 6'2 and had piercing blue eyes with dark blonde hair that was short and mildly unkempt. At the moment, he was just staring blankly into space.

Alexis was the only one who seemed to have her head in the game. Her very light hazel eyes burned with passion, as if she were tired of sitting around. Alexis was only about 5'6 but she wasn't scared of anyone. She had blonde hair that was parted down the middle that day, with a few strands tucked behind her ears so she could see. If my dad had let her, Alexis may have just charged the security guards single handedly.

"Not the greatest group," my dad muttered under his breath, "But they'll do."

The silence soon got the best of Alexis and she was the first to comment on the situation.

"So, does everyone remember the plan?"

Everyone nodded. Then they went to work. Rick grabbed Carrie's hand and, using his ability, he shrank them both down to the size of ballpoint pens. Alexis gently picked up her tiny friends and placed them in the front pocket of her button up shirt then darted towards the mansion with supersonic speed; moving so fast that she was invisible. Alexis blew past the guards with ease, bringing a stiff breeze as she went. When they reached the door, Rick and Carrie returned to their normal size.

"Let's *never* do that again." Rick whispered.

"Agreed." Carrie nodded. She tried the door handle: locked. This would've been a problem…if Carrie didn't have superhuman strength. She crushed the doorknob and launched her palm into the center of the door. Her action ripped the door from the wall and sent it flying into the house but before the door could slam into the floor and wake the owner; Alexis sped off and caught it just in time.

Alexis had succeeded in stopping the door from crashing but when Carrie broke the door off, she alerted the guards.

"Uh-oh." The three friends muttered as the twenty guards charged at them.

"You're up." My dad said to Brody back at the bush.

"Oh. Right. There are *no* guards guarding this mansion." he commanded. Normally, if someone said this, absolutely nothing would happen but Brody was "special" too. He had the power to make anything he said come true. This instance was no different. One by one, the guards began to disappear but then something strange happened. After about ten or eleven guards vanished, a crimson fluid dripped from Brody's nose. His nose was bleeding and he was getting dizzy. The twelfth guard, that was almost completely gone, slowly began to reappear.

"Whoa," Brody said. "What happened? I didn't get them all. Lemme try again." He prepared to repeat his vanishing act, when my dad grabbed his arm firmly.

"If you wish to see your next birthday, you'll stop right now. Your nose is bleeding. Your ability is maxed out and if you push any further, you'll die." He said solemnly.

Xavier had warned us about this last year but no one had gone this far before.

"Timmy," My dad called. "Go."

Timmy nodded, hopped to his feet and started yelling something in an odd language. It sounded like squeaks and other woodland creature sounds. The simplest translation of what he said is: "Hey, everyone! Those guards are made of amazingly tasty acorns!"

There was a dead silence. The remaining guards were looking at Timmy as if he were crazy, then the silence of broken by the sound of scurrying feet. A lot of them. Something I failed to mention before was that a dense, dark forest full of wild animals surrounded the mansion. The scurrying sound turned into full running and moments later, hundreds of squirrels, raccoons, and other furry animals exploded from the woods. Looking very hungry. The animals seized the remaining guards effortlessly and dragged them back into the forest; the guards kicking and screaming as they went. Timmy began to feel bad for the guards but not bad enough to call off his furry friends.

The five friends met up with my dad at the front doorway of the mansion. The guards screaming was faint but could still be heard in the distance. Alexis looked worried.

"Don't worry," Timmy told her. "The animals will figure out that I was lying. Those guys will be fine."

"We need to go now. Preston is very paranoid and frightens easily. Which explains all the security. I'm sure the screaming guards have alerted him by now. We gotta go find him before he runs off with the medallions." My dad explained then took off into the dark building.

"Spread out and find him!" he said in a hushed tone from somewhere in the darkness.

The five teens fanned out and searched vigorously for Preston. This wasn't an easy task. As I said earlier, this was a large mansion and none of them knew what Preston looked like. My dad checked the living room; Brody had the bedrooms and the others swept upstairs and downstairs. They searched for what felt like hours but eventually found the target. Specifically, Brody found him.

Brody's last place to check was the master bedroom. It was dark but Brody could see all he needed to. The room was relatively empty. On the west wall, there were three windows that overlooked the backyard. To the south, there was a large plasma screen TV mounted on the wall. To the east, there was a huge walk-in closet, stuffed with clothes that no respectable person would ever be caught in and on the north wall, there was an enormous king sized canopy bed. And right in the center of the mattress, there was an obvious, human shaped lump, covered in a sheet.

Brody sighed. "Um, I can see you, man." he said.

The sheeted lump wiggled. "Are you here to kill me?" A terrified voice came from the lump.

Brody laughed. "No way, dude. We just need your medallions."

The lump perked up. "That's all?" The lump seemed to be having a seizure of some sort. A few seconds later, it produced a platinum octagon and a titanium cylinder, both on indestructible titanium chains with a golden "C", for Chorifier, on the front.

"They've been more trouble than they're worth." The lump explained. "My team deserted me at the first sign of trouble. We never even fought in a battle. I won this second medallion," He raised the titanium cylinder, "in a poker game."

Brody was grateful but a bit uneasy. "Aren't you afraid of dying? When you hand those over to me, you'll be transported to LIMBO."

The lump shook its head in disagreement. "I'm not afraid of dying as long as it's peaceful. I hired all those guards to protect me from the TBC people who had murder in their hearts. So here," The lump tossed Brody the medallions. "I hope you succeed and win the TBC." The lump said, and then fell flat on the bed.

Brody checked under the sheets for Preston but all he found was sand that slipped away as soon as he uncovered it. Brody replaced the sheets and, with the two newly acquired medallions in hand, he left to rejoin his team.

*****

I was still in shock about the fact that my newfound acquaintances were born with abilities when X called me.

"Hey, X." I said.

"I know where Chris is." he answered back. X never was one for small talk. Even at school, no one really heard him speak. He was much worse on the phone. Straight to the point; never calling just to chat. I'd let it slide this time.

"No way?!" I exclaimed, startling my new friends. "Where is he?"

Xavier proceeded to give me every detail. Then he told me he wanted me to go get Chris myself.

"Sure thing," I told him. "I'll call the rest of the Phalanx and we'll-…"

"No." X cut me off. "This is your task; your test. You can take the fortune manipulator if you wish but no one else. Your plane tickets will be waiting at the airport. Hurry."

The line went dead. Xavier had hung up on me. The fortune manipulator? He must be talking about Kyle. But how did X know about him? What's more confusing is how he said my *tickets* would be waiting instead of my *ticket* as if he knew I'd have company. Then again, he probably did know; he could see the future after all. I put away my phone and Kyle asked if something was wrong.

"No," I said. "I just have to visit an old friend. Wanna come?"

Kyle and I arrived at the airport, with our carry-on luggage; we didn't expect to be gone long. We picked up our tickets and grabbed a nearby seat in the waiting area of Gate 7, hoping our section of the plane would be called soon. I fumbled with my ticket anxiously as I sat. I wondered what I'd say to Chris when I saw him again.

"Section B, rows 31 through 60 are now boarding flight 320, non-stop to Hamilton." the stewardess called over the loudspeaker in an overly cheery voice.

"That's us." Kyle commented eagerly. We boarded the plane and found our seats. We sat in row 33. It was just the two of us in the row, so we got comfortable and waited for the plane to take off. On the ground below, the airline employees were hard at work, loading the luggage into the cargo hold. So busy, in fact, that they failed to notice three invisible freeloaders sneak into the hold. The workers felt a slight breeze as the three invisible teens ran by but they didn't think much of it. The men finished and shut the cargo hold's door tightly.

Inside the plane, the stewardess began to demonstrate how to properly fasten a seatbelt, how to use the overhead mask, et cetera, et cetera. They were wasting their time though. No one was paying attention. The fasten seatbelt symbol illuminated above our heads and the pilot announced that all electronic devices needed to be turned off. Then we were airborne. Take off was kinda shaky but I didn't have many complaints. The plane leveled off at around 30,000 feet.

*****

"Are we there yet?" Danny asked, trying to be funny. No one laughed.

"We shouldn't talk too much. I'm pretty sure riding in the cargo hold of a plane is hazardous to your health." Sarita lectured. "I'm using my ability to convert our carbon dioxide into oxygen but we still need to conserve our air. This is going to be a long flight." Sarita's ability to manipulate nature allowed her to do things like that. Danny knew Sarita was right so he didn't say another word. Neither did Hannah. *Hamilton, here we come*, he thought.

*****

We had been flying for a few hours when Kyle asked: "Where are we going, anyway?"

"Hamilton." I said, as if it wasn't completely obvious.

"No, I know that. But where is that? Like, what state is it in?"

I laughed. "It's not in the United States. It's in Bermuda. Why do you think we needed our passports?"

A grave look washed over Kyle's face as if I had just told him his mom died.

"What's wrong?" I asked, genuinely concerned.

"I need to get off this plane." He muttered.

"What?"

"I *need* to get off this plane." He said louder, trying to remain calm.

"Why? What's going on? Do you have something against Bermuda?"

He shook his head. "Not Bermuda. But a certain triangle that surrounds it."

'The Bermuda Triangle?" I asked, surprised. "Isn't that just a story? It can't be real."

"A person who can create fire and lightning with his bare hands can't be real either and yet here you are, sitting right next to me."

He had a point.

"Ok. I get it. But what's so bad about the Bermuda Triangle? Only ships disappear in it. We're 30,000 feet in the air; I think we'll be fine." I joked. Kyle didn't laugh.

"You don't understand!" He explained, trying to keep his voice down. "The Bermuda Triangle does...something to my power."

Now, I was listening. "What kind of 'something'?"

"It magnifies the misfortune side of my ability. I lose all control of what happens. Something small could happen like spilling hot coffee on your lap or something huge like..."

"...the plane going down." I finished his sentence. He nodded. "We have to get you off this plane!" I parroted and the look on his face said, *Duh!*

I waved for the stewardess' attention but she was preoccupied with another passenger. They were flirting hardcore.

This is so not the time! I thought.

Kyle was hyperventilating next to me and it was started to make me nervous.

"Excuse me!" I yelled down the aisle for the flight attendants attention.

"Shhh! Sir, I'll be with you in a second!" She hissed and went back to her conversation.

Overhead, I saw the "Call Attendant" button. I pressed it repeated. No response.

"This is the worst service ever! Do you guy *want* to die?!" I seethed under my breath.

After the stewardess appeared to write her number down on the passenger's hand, she deliberately walked slowly towards me; periodically peering over her shoulder to see if the male passenger was looking at her. They met eyes each time and, each time, she turned away quickly and giggled.

Really? Is this high school?

The flight attendant finally reached my seat.

"How can I help you, *sir?*" She asked, with emphasis on the "sir". She was clearly annoyed that I interrupted her oh-so-important conversation with a guy that was probably never going to call her.

I began to ramble hysterically about how we had to land the plane as soon as possible but it was too late. The pilot came over the loudspeaker once again.

"Attention all passengers. This is your captain speaking. We will be arriving in Hamilton, Bermuda shortly. We are about 100 miles away right now. Also, just a little fun fact, we've just entered the fabled *Bermuda Triangle*," He imitated ghost noises after he said Bermuda Triangle.

"Hopefully," he continued, "the rumors about the Triangle aren't true and we land safely." The laughter of the Pilot and Co-pilot could be heard from the cockpit. A giggle or two could be heard in the cabin. They all thought this was just a joke. If only it were.

They won't be laughing for long, I thought. Shortly after the announcement, the cabin lights began to flicker then they blew out completely and the plane itself started to shake violently. The rude flight attendant was thrown in the air by heavy turbulence and slammed into the floor.

A panic quickly swept through the cabin.

Everyone was screaming, unbuckling their seat belts and running around in the cabin.

Progression

As if they could go anywhere else.
This is exactly what I was trying to prevent.
I'm not gonna lie, I was freaking out a bit myself.
Kyle leaned over the armrest and whispered, somberly: "This is only the beginning."

Chapter 17

"Elevation"

Elevation: To lift up or make higher; to improve morally,

intellectually, or culturally

So, to recap, on my way to find my friend Chris, our plane malfunctioned (thanks to Kyle) and now we're about to crash. I wasn't the best at Geography but I think we were over the Atlantic Ocean. When things first started going to hell, Danny, Sarita, and Hannah fell out of the sky with the luggage when the cargo hold broke open. Kyle and I would be killed if we didn't do the same. Two parachute packs slid from the cockpit to my feet.

"We have to jump!" I yelled over the sound of rushing wind.

"Are you crazy?!" he asked.

I shook my head. "It's the only way!" And we strapped up the packs, closed our eyes, and leaped.

Had the situation been different, this skydiving experience would've been very fun. I had always imagined what skydiving would feel like but I never thought it would feel like this. Time seemed to slow down as we plummeted from the sky. There's no falling sensation; the closest thing I can compare it to is swimming. You're completely surrounded and yet you're free to move around. My breathing was forced and difficult with all the air rushing up my nose and into my mouth. My eyes were watering badly as I tried to look at everything around me.

Probably should've brought goggles, I thought.

Kyle was a few feet above me. I waved at him as if we were just skydiving for fun. He was frantically yelling something but I couldn't hear it. The wind was too loud. I tried to read his lips. It took a second but I figured out most of what he was saying: *Look out. Here comes a train.* A train? In the sky? No, the last word looked like train but it wasn't. And when I finally understood, it was too late. About 20 feet below me, a passenger plane was coming from the opposite direction of our crashing plane and in a few seconds, I'd be splattered on the windshield of the oncoming plane.

I panicked and pulled my parachute cord but not soon enough. The parachute slowed my free fall but my parachute strings got tangled on the right wing of the passenger plane. The momentum of the plane yanked me from my original trajectory and slammed me into the under belly of the plane, knocking me unconscious. The plane continued on its path, dragging me along with it, heading back to where flight 320 started to go down.

*****

Meanwhile, Derrick was still the only one stuck in the first phase of Limbo. He and the illusion of his younger self were having a long conversation.

"I guess...I don't know. I think I resent my family for letting my little brother compete in the TBC with me. I know we're twins and all but I was born first, you know?" The young Derrick nodded in agreement. "I didn't mean to hurt anyone. Especially not my friends but the desire to win and beat Xavier consumed me."

Derrick paused. "I really messed up, didn't I?" he asked.

"Well, yeah. You kinda did. But it's not too late. Go. Join your team; help them escape Limbo, then make amends with everyone else."

"How? That's so much to do. Where do I start?" The real Derrick asked.

The young Derrick just smiled and said: "Start at the beginning."

The illusion vanished and everything around Derrick went dark. The light returned and Derrick noticed he wasn't in the same room as before. He was now surrounded by sandstone walls that were spaced about 10 feet apart, were 15 feet high and snaked in various directions as far as the eye could see; forming a complicated labyrinth that seemed to be endless.

To Derrick's surprise, he wasn't alone. Jayden, Staci, Curt, and Jared were lost in the labyrinth too. Before Derrick could begin to apologize, a deep, menacing growl emanated from behind the teens. There were two huge dogs staring hungrily at the five friends. They looked like Rottweilers only four times larger. Their eye sockets were empty and there were flames where their eyes should've been. The dogs were drooling excessively, seeming to size up the teens, deciding whom to eat first.

Everyone was frozen with fear. "Guys," Derrick said, shakily. "You have no reason to trust me after all I've done to you but I promise I can redeem myself if you just do as I say. *Please*."

The four remaining members of the Legion nodded silently. "Ok, Derrick." Jared said, "But these dogs are pretty big. I don't know if we can take them. Where would we even start?"

Derrick remembered advice that he was given a little earlier. Derrick just smiled and said: "Start at the beginning." A dagger mysteriously materialized in his hand then he lunged at the nearest hellhound.

*****

I don't remember what happened after my parachute got caught on the wing of the plane. I dreamt that my parachute strings broke and I fell into the Atlantic Ocean, but when I woke up, I was floating in the water so I reasoned my dream was pretty accurate. I was floating on the cushion of a seat from the airplane but I'm not sure where I got it from.

The water was cold and denser than the Ocean water should be. It made wading difficult. The breeze was salty and the clouds overhead looked ominous. A storm was coming and I needed to get to safety before that happened or I'd drown. Only one question: which way was safety? I swam in circles looking for some type of land or boat or...something. But there was nothing; just ocean as far as the eye could see.

Then I thought about something: Where was Kyle? I frantically searched for him but he was nowhere in sight. How far did that plane take me? I dove underwater and looked. I only lasted a few seconds, the water was too much for my eyes; too salty.

I hope he's alright, I thought. I wished Kyle luck wherever he was then swam northwest. Or at least I figured it was northwest. It's so hard to tell without the sun. I figured I'd hit land eventually. I swam and took a break then swam and took a break, along with my trusty floatation device/cushion, for what felt like days but was probably only an hour or two. Then I spotted something. Or someone. Actually, it was three someones. Ugh. That's bad grammar. Anyway, on my way to...wherever, I ran into three people. They were floating on luggage from flight 320. I knew this because I could vaguely see the tags on the suitcases. There was a white guy, a black girl, and a Hispanic girl. They had to have been around my age but I couldn't see their faces. I had to see if they were ok. More importantly, I needed to find out if they knew where we were. As I hurried toward the survivors, it began to rain, slowly at first but then more steadily. The wind kicked in as well and the combination blew me in the wrong direction repeatedly. But I wasn't deterred. I dug in deep and pushed on to the three teens.

After quite a bit of struggling with nature, I arrived, exhausted, at my destination. I reached for the guy first. He was lying on the suitcase, face down but there was still something familiar about him. The teen awoke with a start when I shook his shoulder.

"Where am I?!" Danny exclaimed, almost falling off his luggage.

"That's a great question. What are you even doing here?" I asked.

Danny sighed then proceeded to tell me the entire story: The letter, the secrecy, the stowing away, everything. The rain was pouring and the wind was screaming so Danny had to yell most of the time but I got the important details.

"Where are Hannah and Sarita?!" I asked over the hiss of the wind. Danny pointed to the two girls I saw earlier. They were awake now and very disoriented.

"Where are we?" was the question I saw Sarita mouth to Hannah. Hannah shook her head then spotted Danny and me. She pointed at us and we swam over, they met us halfway. We were all drenched and freezing but alive. We were very thankful for that much but our reunion was cut short by a huge tidal wave, 50 feet high at least. Hannah, Sarita and I were frozen with fear but Danny was just as alert as ever. He morphed into a blue whale and sucked everyone into his mouth moments before the wave crashed down on us.

Danny's whale form was taking a severe beating from the ocean but it was nothing compared to what we were going through in his mouth. Hannah, Sarita, and I tumbled around in Danny's saliva filled mouth like we were delicates in a dryer. I'd rather not go into detail but let's just say I never wanted to be inside his mouth again. That, and Danny really needed to brush better.

After about a lifetime of bouncing uncomfortably on Danny's tongue, things finally settled down.

"Hey guys!" Danny's voice bellowed from his throat, echoing in his mouth. "I think we're here!"

He opened his mouth and we peeked out. None of us had been to Bermuda before but there weren't many options as to what this island in front of us could be. We could vaguely make out buildings. They weren't huge but they proved that people lived there.

Danny spit us all out-along with the luggage and my floatation seat-and then changed back to his human state. He looked exhausted but we made it. The island that we assumed to be Bermuda was maybe five miles away. The rain had died down, the sky was clear, the sun was shining and the wind was calm. I took a deep breath then a lump rose in my throat.

"Hey Danny," I squeaked.

"Yeah?"

"What are the chances of you turning into a whale again? Like now?"

"No can do," He said. "I'm maxed out and I'd prefer not to die."

"I don't think you have a choice in the matter." I muttered, solemnly.

"What do you..." As Danny was speaking, a giant shadow was cast over us. Something very large was blocking our sunlight. No one looked right away because we knew what it was. A monstrous wave, larger than anything I had seen before, was seconds from taking our lives. It had to have been 150 to 200 feet high.

"It was nice knowing you guys," said Danny, then everyone closed their eyes and mentally prepared for death.

I hadn't known it then, but I would never see Kyle again. While my parachute strings had dragged me back to Bermuda, Kyle drifted on, maneuvering his chute like a trained pro. He landed somewhere near the Florida Keys and left his parachute on the beach. Kyle surveyed his surroundings. It was a beautiful day out but the beach was desolate. *Probably because of that storm*, he thought. The storm he was referring to just so happened to be the storm my friends and I were caught in.

Kyle walked around the beach in search of something. He kicked up sand and overturned rocks as he looked. After a few minutes of searching, he seemed to have found "it". The "it" in question was a bronze sand dollar with a silver "D" etched into the surface. Kyle dusted off the sand dollar, turned it clockwise by 180 degrees, then the ground came to life. A portal opened up in front of him and sand spilled onto stairs below.

Kyle headed down the sandy stairs and the door closed behind him. The stairs began to spiral as he walked deeper into the darkness. The passageway opened up to a huge storage warehouse. Saw dust scattered in a thin layer on the floor and the distinct scent of pine trees filled the air.

The warehouse was dimly lit; the only sources of light came from the light bulbs suspended from the ceilings, spaced a few yards a part. Wooden crates lined the walls on the left and right, climbing up to the rafters.

Towards the end of the warehouse, there were two thrones, with a man and a woman occupying them. Kyle squinted to see the physical features of the couple but it was too dark. He stepped closer for a better look.

"That's far enough!" The woman stated in a distorted voice and Kyle froze in his tracks, like magic.

"Do you have the DNA?" She asked. Kyle remained still. The woman frowned. "Speak!" she demanded.

"Yes. I got it. From all five of them." Kyle reached into his pockets and pulled out five tiny plastic bags; each contained a few strands of hair in them and they were all labeled: Chris. Sarita. Danny. Frankie. Hannah. How did Kyle get our hair? And why did this lady need it?

"Excellent," The man said, also with a distorted voice. "And the plane crash?"

"It went according to plan, sir. Frankie believed it was an accident." Kyle told them.

"Well done, boy." The woman complimented him. "Where is young Franklin?"

Kyle hesitated. "I, kinda, lost him on the way down..." Kyle flinched because he knew they wouldn't like this news.

"What?!" They hissed simultaneously. "Unacceptable!" The woman clenched her fist and Kyle's body went stiff as a board.

"You've served us well, Kyle," the woman whispered seductively. "But D.A.N.S.H.A. is no longer in need of your services." Tears streamed down Kyle's face but he remained

56

silent and motionless. Whatever they were doing to him, he wasn't enjoying it.

A disturbing smile crept across the woman's face. "Goodbye." She laughed and, with a swish of her finger, Kyle crumbled to the floor, lifeless. Just like that, Kyle was dead. He may have been a traitor but no one deserved that.

"That was twisted, Priscilla." the man stated, pretending to be disgusted.

"But Francisco, isn't that why you love me?" she asked, innocently.

Francisco gave here a cold smile and kissed her hand. "Right you are," he agreed then whistled sharply into the darkness. A hologram appeared shortly after. The hologram resembled a slightly pudgy blonde haired girl with sky blue eyes and an innocent smile. She wore a well fitting business suit that made her look older than she was supposed to. She was probably programmed to look about 17 or 18 but her attire said 20 or 21.

"Computer," Francisco began, "Summon Isaiah Lamberg. He needs to be…judged." There was a bit of spite in his voice as if he had a personal problem with my dad. "Also, take these bags to the lab and begin the cloning process. We need the clones up and running as soon as possible." The hologram nodded then vanished; the bags disappeared with it.

*****

We waited for death…but it didn't come. We floated there for about a minute and nothing happened. I cautiously opened one eye and I couldn't believe what I saw. A wall of porous rock stood as high as a skyscraper, protecting us from the wrath of the ocean. I nudged my friends and they saw it too.

"Who did this? How?" Hannah stuttered.
"Who do you think?" answered a voice from behind us. We all turned to see a Mexican teenage boy standing on a surfboard made of limestone. He was pretty buff with huge, muscular arms and legs. He had light brown skin and hazel eyes with jet-black hair that was usually spiked up with gel but the ocean water had washed it all out. He wore a navy blue wetsuit with the words

"Oceania Mobile" on his chest. The teen smiled and we couldn't help but do the same. It was Chris Flores and I had never been happier to see him.

Chapter 18

"Reformation"

Reformation: To amend or improve by change of form or

removal of faults or abuses.

The hellhounds were the least of the Legion's worries. In the labyrinth, they faced dog-sized scorpions with titanium stingers, man eating Venus flytraps (Venus man traps, if you will), and other unspeakable things. The air was stale with the stench of death and everyone was beginning to get claustrophobic. Derrick had just vanquished some kind of vampire-werewolf hybrid when an illusion of David appeared in front of him. Still in battle mode, Derrick slashed at it, instinctively. His dagger phased harmlessly through the hologram, disturbing the picture momentarily.

"That's not necessary, Derrick," David's illusion smirked. "I mean you no harm. You five have done very well and I'm here to offer you a choice."

David had everyone's attention.

"What choice?" Staci asked.

"I can send you back to reality, or you can stay here." he told the team. The five friends just stared at David's illusion like he was crazy.

"That's a no brainer..." Curt started to say but David cut him off.

"Before you decide, look where we are."

The Legion did as they were told and soon realized they were no longer in a dark maze but an amusement park. The air was still and the sun was shining as the rides operated by themselves. The park was abandoned.

"If you haven't figured it out by now, L.I.M.B.O. is just a virtual reality program. I am the programmer. And as such, I can take you guys anywhere you want to go." David explained.

"But this isn't real..." Jared said. David's illusion just laughed and a crème pie formed in his hand. He threw the pie before anyone could react and it nailed Jared in the face. The pan slid down his face and fell to the floor.

"It's real enough." David added. "The monsters you just faced were real enough to hit you and that pie is real enough to keep you nourished. As is anything I create for you."

To demonstrate, David took the friends to Times Square. Taxis flew by them, dragging yesterday's newspaper in their wake. Just as quickly as it had been there, Times Square melted away and was replaced by the Hollywood Walk of Fame. Then London. Egypt. Hawaii. Australia. Each place felt as real as humanly possible.

"Everyone can live their dream life. Right here. Right now. No restrictions. No limitations. Just think it and it is yours. Forget about your old life. Forget about the TBC. Forget about your friends. This is your chance to start over." David's illusion seemed satisfied with the looks of amazement on everyone's face. "So, what do you say?"

*****

"No!" Chris said firmly. He wasn't budging. Chris refused to come back home with us.

"Why not?!" Danny exclaimed. "We need each other, dude! We're so close to winning it!" Hannah put her hand on Danny's shoulder and he cooled off a bit.

"What about your parents?" Hannah asked.

"They know I'm here." By "here", he meant his rich uncle's beach house in Bermuda. We were all relaxing on the beach, trying to persuade Chris. We had been here for two months and we hadn't made any headway. We were missing school but my mom and David had taken care of that with some lie about a foreign exchange program (I'm not sure about the details but it was believable). The setting sun colored the ocean a bright crimson tone as if it were on fire.

Chris sighed. "We should get going. The tide will be coming in soon." Then, without another word, he retired to the beach house, slamming the screen door behind him.

I was restless that night. But I quickly found out that I wasn't the only one. As I laid in the ridiculously lumpy twin sized bed, I began to hear noises on the roof; footsteps to be exact. I rolled to the left to see the digital clock on the nightstand next to my bed. 1:13 A.M. glowed in red. I slid out of the bed, careful not to wake my slumbering team members. I stepped outside, barefoot, stood on the porch and just listened. It was silent except for the sound of the ocean water gliding over the moist sand then retreating shortly after. That's when I heard it again. Someone was definitely pacing on the roof. I really didn't need to look to know who it was. I circled the house until I figured out how he got up there then followed his example. The roof was flatter than my roof back home but it was just as easy to climb.

I reached the top quickly to find Chris, no longer pacing, on the roof. He was now sitting, feet dangling over the edge, looking more lost than I had ever seen him. Now, I'll admit, Chris and I have never exactly been friends but it killed me to see him like this. I sat next to Chris, startling him a bit.

"I kinda figured it would be you to come up here first." he whispered, staring out into space. "You always were the closest to me, personality wise and following a strange noise is something I would do." Chris laughed lightly. "I guess that's why I was always competing with you. We were so close that I felt the need to prove that I was better than you. But now I don't feel that way anymore. I've done a lot of growing up since-" He choked on his words. "Well, you know."

I nodded. "Yeah. I know. That wasn't your fault." I told him, reassuringly.

"Maybe not but that doesn't change the fact that she's gone but by not coming back with you guys, I can guarantee I never hurt anyone else again." He said then got lost in his thought again.

I was losing him. I needed to think of something quick.

"Who will protect us if you're not there?" I asked, stroking Chris' ego. "I mean, you really saved our lives when we first got here. That wave would've wiped us out if you hadn't been there. This whole TBC thing is so dangerous. We could use all the help we can get."

"I dunno." he said, absently. I had him. Time to reel him in.

"Laura would've wanted you to finish."

Chris perked up at the mention of his lost girlfriend's name.

"She would?" he asked.

"Of course. Plus, if we win, there are those three rule free wishes. One could be to bring Laura back." I didn't have to ask what his answer was. Chris slid excitedly off the roof; a feat that was impossible to do without injury, but Chris' ability spared him any pain. He manipulated the sand below into cushioning his fall. Sometimes, I envy the guy. And other times...

"What are you waiting for?!" He called from below. "Let's get going!"

Meanwhile, stateside, my dad had been summoned by D.A.N.S.H.A. and it wasn't looking good for him.

"Why isn't he dead?" Priscilla asked, impatiently.

"I'm sorry. There were...complications." He stated, firmly.

"From your wife?" Francisco added.

"Ex-wife," Priscilla continued. My dad was speechless.

Priscilla laughed. "What? You didn't think we knew about your marriage to Elizabeth? Or your son, Franklin? Did you think we didn't know you were a spy?" Priscilla cackled. "No, we knew. We know all. Thanks to my husband's ability,

D.A.N.S.H.A. knows everything that has happened, everything that is happening, and everything that will happen. We played dumb because it was profitable for us to do so. But that is no longer the case. Now, if you don't do exactly as we say, we will kill everything and everyone you care about." Priscilla sat back in her throne, content with what she had said.

My dad sighed. "Alright," he muttered, shoulders slumped, looking defeated in more ways than one. "What do you want me to do?"

Francisco snapped his fingers and my friends and I stepped out of the shadows. This was impossible because my friends and I were still in Bermuda. D.A.N.S.H.A. had successfully cloned the members of the Phalanx, down to every detail: From the gap in my front teeth to the scar on Danny's eyebrow.

"Do?" Francisco repeated, curiously. "We don't want you to 'do' anything. We want you to do absolutely nothing as we destroy your son and his friends."

My dad sized up the clones. They all had vacant stares on their faces as if they weren't fully "there". My dad was torn. If he let them go, the clones would try to kill me and my friends. But if he stopped them, D.A.N.S.H.A. would definitely kill us. He had to choose the lesser of two evils. The decision was obvious but he couldn't let us go into this blindly.

Without notice, my dad whipped out his phone, typed out a text, and pressed "send" before Priscilla realized what he was doing.

"Hey!" she yelled and used her ability to make my dad crush his phone. "You didn't say he would try and warn them!" Priscilla hissed at Francisco.

"I told you it was a possibility! Being omniscient means I know everything that *could* happen in the present and future. Him trying to warn the kids changes the outcome of the situation." Francisco spat back.

"We need to send the clones now before we lose the element of surprise." Priscilla reasoned and turned to the clones.

"You know your objectives. Now, go!" She demanded. The cloned Phalanx obeyed and hurried off into the darkness.

"And as for you," Priscilla sneered; now focusing on my dad. "You'll rot in the dungeon. Currently, since you've collected five medallions, you're worth more alive than dead. You'd better hope nothing happens to change that."

Priscilla summoned guards and they dragged my dad away to the dungeon an unseen part of the warehouse.

*****

"Do we have everything?" Hannah asked everyone.

We all nodded. We were packed up and ready to head back home.

"Did everyone go to the restroom?" Sarita nagged.

"Yes, *Mother*." Danny groaned.

We were all traveling pretty light considering everything we brought with us had been washed away.

Chris put the spare key back under the welcome mat and we were about to head out when my phone vibrated. (This should've been impossible because my phone was damaged beyond repair from our "swim" in the Atlantic Ocean.) Or so I thought.

I stared at my pocket with a stupefied look on my face then checked the message. My screen was filled with water but I could barely make out what it said.

"Who's it from?" Danny wondered, just as surprised as I was that the phone was more than an expensive paperweight after what it had been through.

"My dad," I told him, blankly.

"Well…what's it say?" Sarita asked.

I tried to wipe off moisture from the screen and read it out loud.

Everyone crowded around me, genuinely curious as to what my dad would have to say. I had to reread the text multiple times, it made absolutely no sense.

Could this be right? I thought.

"It says…" I squinted to interpret the text message. "Attack of the Clones."

Chapter 19

"Self-Destruction"

Self-Destruction: The act of destroying one's self.

I didn't understand my dad's warning until it was too late. I was standing in line at the airport fast food chain when someone shoved me. Hard. I stumbled into a heavy set Asian woman in front of me, bounced off of her as if her fat was a trampoline, and skidded along the linoleum floor. I sprang to my feet; ready to fight until I saw who it was that pushed me. It wasn't possible. I shouldn't say that considering everything I've seen this past year or two but, all things considered, this was pretty strange. I looked to see who the culprit was and I saw...myself. It was like looking in a mirror.

"Clone," I said under my breath. The clone's hands began to sizzle then erupted into white flames. He smirked at me. "Whoa. Angry clone." I muttered and rolled out of the way as he launched white-hot fireballs in my direction.

The shots narrowly missed me, flew over the counter of the fast food restaurant, and landed in the kitchen. Now, you can imagine what happens when fire lands in a grease covered kitchen... Danny found out the hard way last year when he burned down the Remington Estate. The same thing happened here. An explosion could be heard from the back, the grease traps had caught on fire and exploded. Screaming fry cooks fled the flames as it consumed the restaurant.

That was the point when all hell broke loose. The fire sprinklers came to life, dousing anything and everything in the area but the grease fire burned on because grease and water don't mix. The heavyset Asian woman I bumped into was the first to scream and everyone else followed her example. Those waiting in line scattered for the nearest exits, spreading panic in all directions. It's funny how no one ever handles situations like these as calmly as they should.

Stem rose from my clothes as I tried to dry off.

"This will surely draw the attention of cops. I need to make this quick." I mumbled. Apparently, my clone was thinking the same thing because he charged at me, full force. I rolled to the side and he crashed into a table, smashing it to pieces.

He's not very bright, I thought. The clone rose to his feet and his hands began to glow again. He formed a flame in his hand that was so hot, it evaporated all the falling water around him. The fire grew until it was the size of a basketball then he threw it at me.

I know this wasn't the smartest idea I've ever had, but, as the ball approached, I put my hands out as if to block it. I don't know what was stranger: my idea to block fire with my bare hands or the fact that it actually worked. No joke. When the flaming projectile reached me, I caught it.

Oh, duh, I thought. *I manipulate fire, so it can't hurt me.* I considered throwing it back but it wouldn't have done any good since he could do everything I could. Or could he? The clone seemed to lack common sense, so maybe he hadn't learned about lightning…it was worth a shot. But how could I use this to my advantage?

The sprinklers continued to rain down on us and I remembered how I defeated Jared last year but for this to work, I'd need a lot more water.

"Thanks for this!" I called to him. "It was getting a little chilly." I knew it wasn't smart but I'd hoped he could be baited into attacking me. Turns out, he could. He ran at me again, hands blazing. I tossed the fireball overhead and it hit a sprinkler; which pumped out more water in response.

The clone swung at me with his right fist but I quickly deflected his blow upward. A wave of fire darted from his fist towards the ceiling and more water poured down on us. He attempted the same move again and again, with the same results. Swing, miss, blast above, and water came down.

The clone was getting worn down pretty quickly so I decided it was time to finish this. I crouched down and, with one clean swept of my foot, knocked him off his feet and he slammed on the floor. I created some distance between us and, while he gathered his wits, I charged a lightning bolt behind my back.

"Oh, come on now. That can't be all you've got. Tell you what, I'll fight you with one hand." I waved my free hand. "Sound good?" I laughed. Which was my first mistake. My second mistake was underestimating how fast my clone was. He was so angry and came at me faster than I had ever seen, then lunged at me. If I hadn't been laughing, I might've been more prepared for it. But he caught me off guard and I fired the lightning bolt in a panic. *That* was my third mistake.

The clone had gotten so close to me that, when I extended my arm to fire, I touched him. I had no time to absorb the blow and when I shot him, I shocked myself as well. The jolt sent us flying in opposite directions and crashing into the ground. We laid there, unconscious, as the sprinklers continued to pour, unphased. After about a minute or two, I woke up. Seeing the clone still passed out, I used this as an opportunity to make my getaway and find my friends.

*****

Danny wasn't having much luck with his clone. He fought hard, not smart and his foe was matching him blow for blow. Their constant fighting had brought them to baggage claim. Danny's duplicate was in the form of a massive anaconda and it slung bag after bag at the real Danny with ridiculous speed but Danny, who shifted to a mule, kicked away each item with ease. They were both getting pretty worn down. Danny had gone through dozens of transformations and Xavier's grave warning

68

from a year ago was buzzing in the back of his mind: *using your power for a prolonged period of time could get you stuck that way forever.*

Definitely not, He thought and changed back to his human form.

"Hey ugly!" Danny yelled. "Catch me if you can!" Then morphed into a calico cat and darted off. The clone sprang after him, in the form of a German shepherd. Danny was slipping and sliding on the slick floor, wet from the sprinkler system, with his canine foe right on his tail. Literally. The dog gnashed at Danny's tail, barely missing. Without hesitation, Danny morphed into a Finch and shot into the air. He looked back and saw a dragonfly in fast pursuit.

Time to go smaller, he thought and shrunk to a horsefly while continuing his evasive maneuvering. The dragonfly was much faster than Danny but it was all a part of his plan. When the clone was a second away from Danny, Danny transformed into a lemur, grabbed the dragonfly as tight as he could and they plummeted to the floor. The ground was coming fast and, moments before impact, Danny let go of the bug and landed safely on the ground while his clone smashed into the tile.

Danny was human again and his opponent was down for the count. The dragonfly looked pretty mangled and in pain but it still struggled to move. The dragonfly began to change to his human form but it stopped halfway and regressed to its insect state.

"Bingo. Don't bother getting up, bud. You've exhausted your ability. Simply put, you're stuck." Danny raised his foot over the clones head. He planned to end it all right there but, instead, he was rather pleased with himself and walked away, triumphantly.

In my hurried state, I ran into Danny and we both fell to the floor. We sprang to our feet, ready to fight then let out a loud sigh of relief when we recognized each other. Our reunion was cut short by a feminine scream coming from the restroom.

The door to the women's restroom had been ripped off the hinges by wild vines as thick as tree trunks. The entrance to the restroom was so congested with greenery; it was impossible to see through.

"How are we gonna get through?" Danny asked me. I just winked and my hands ignited in flames. He smiled at me. "I like the way you think." he said and his hands turned into giant machete blades.

"That's new." I commented, nonchalantly.

"I've been practicing." He laughed and attacked the vines like they were paper-thin. He vanished into the jungle in moments, the sound of slicing echoed back to me.

"That's the spirit." I called ahead and scorched my way through the dense vines.

Inside, the lights were dim because various shrubs blocked most of the fluorescent lighting. Danny and I cut and burned our way through our obstacles until we reached the middle stall. The door was locked but Danny ripped through it with ease. The shredded pieces fell to the ground and revealed a tangled Sarita; trapped in a tree that sprouted from where the toilet should've been. The trunk consumed her entire body and the only part of her that was recognizable was her face. A tree branch had grown horizontally across her face, successfully gagging her mouth.

Sarita made a sad attempt to communicate but it failed. There was an obvious look of urgency in her eyes.

"What?" Danny wondered. He made quick work of the tree and Sarita's gag. She spit out wood chips and nodded her gratitude.

Sarita brushed off a few stray wood chips briskly and exclaimed, "It was a trap!" I didn't have time to react before a flash of green whizzed by and knocked me through a row of stalls nearby.

Disoriented and confused, I was helpless to resist as Sarita's clone lowered itself from the ceiling and wrapped me so tight in vines that I could barely breathe. I had about 30 seconds to live.

What am I doing? I thought. My whole body burst into flames, incinerating the makeshift ropes almost instantly. I hopped to my feet and shot a glance at Danny. He just nodded. He knew what was next and, without a word, we charged the clone; flames flying and blades swinging.

Danny was fighting off the vines as fast as he could but clone was too fast. Danny slashed two in front of him and then a fist shaped one hit him from behind. He sliced at the fist, but it was too quick and he was punched in the stomach, then the face, then was pinned again the wall.

Before delivering the final blow, I raised a fiery wall between Danny and his assailant. The flames burned the clone's ties on my friend and pushed her backwards; right into Sarita's trap.

"Thought I'd return the favor!" she joked as the clone was strung up by her feet and cocooned like a caterpillar waiting to become a beautiful butterfly. Congratulatory handshakes and fist bumps were exchanged. We were so distracted that we failed to see the toilet seat rising into the air on its own. Sarita was about to be cracked over the head with the porcelain toilet seat when Hannah screamed, "Look out!" The toilet seat jolted from the air and shattered on the ground. Hannah's clone had been lurking around the airport, invisible but Hannah had finally caught up with her. Hannah tackled her clone and it was now visible and out cold from a blow to the head.

"Hannah!" We cheered but, again, or celebrations were limited by a huge earthquake. We didn't have to ask because we already knew who it was: Chris.

Actually, it was his clone. Chris had, believe it or not, outsmarted his clone and the copy was flipping out. He was in self-destruct mode. He seemed to have the mentality that, if he wasn't going to win, no one would and he was determined to bring down the entire terminal. And he was succeeding.

71

We needed to go.

"Come on, guys!" Chris screamed over the rumbling as he sprinted into the women's restroom. He was out of breath from running all over the airport, looking for us. "We gotta go!"

He didn't have to tell us twice. The five of us barreled through the restroom door and poured into the main terminal. We ran faster than ever before, dodging falling signs and deflecting random flying objects.

Luck, fate, destiny and all other forms of good fortune must've been on our side because we escaped with no more than half a second to spare. The structure collapsed and a cloud of dust flew into the sky. The air was thick with dirt and it was difficult to see three feet in front of us.

The rubble near my feet shook a bit and two medallions, a Golden egg and a Silver rectangle, appeared from underneath then vanished just as quickly; no doubt traveling to Xavier back in Texas. The meaning of this didn't hit us immediately but we soon understood.

We had done it. We had all five medallions. We were in the semi-finals for the TBC. All of our hard work had paid off. It was a bit rocky getting here, but we had done it together.

My friends and I smiled goofily at each other.

"Oh yeah!" We cheered.

You'd think that, considering the events of the past few hours, we'd be wise enough to know that celebrating only brought trouble. This instance was no different. Police sirens whistled and cops soon surrounded us.

Apparently, someone called the cops and described our clones as terrorists or something. But, with our doppelgangers nowhere in site, my friends and I were the next best thing. Actually, we were the only "thing". There was no way we could explain this. We've never been so screwed in our young lives!

"Freeze! Put your hands in the air!" One of the cops ordered through a megaphone.

"Oh, no…" We groaned as the cops pulled out their cuffs, arrested each of us, then slid us roughly into their backseats.

Chapter 20

"Incarceration"

Incarceration: To put in prison; to subject to confinement.

Words of advice: Never go to prison. It sucks. There was no trial, no holding rooms, and no "one phone call". It all seemed suspect to me. Was this how things were run in Bermuda? The prison was co-ed and about four to five acres but I could be wrong. The grounds were unkempt and there was thick dust in the air. I assumed major construction was underway somewhere close by. The building was in dire need of a paint job. For a prison, it wasn't as intimidating as I figured it would be (it had nothing on my huge high school).

They split us all up into different cells, so I had no idea where my friends were. I don't know about everyone else, but my cell was disgusting. Like seriously vile. The guard pushed me into it and I fell onto the moist, almost slimy floor. There was a distinct stench of feces and urine emanating from the toilet in the far left corner of my cell. It was poorly lit but I could make out bunk beds on the east wall. There was already a prisoner on the top bunk, lying on his side with his back to me.

Immediately, I began to panic. What was he in for? Arson? Robbery? Murder? I shivered at the thought. I didn't wanna know.

"Here," The guard threw me an orange jumpsuit similar to the one my dad gave Danny last year so that he wasn't naked when he returned to his human form. There were odd stains on the suit but I slid it on anyway. The guard nodded, satisfied and, after I handed him my old clothes, he slammed the cell shut and left.

I needed to get out of here. My new "roommate" seemed to be sleeping so he wouldn't notice a melted cell door. I focused on burning "hot" not "bright" then laid my hands on the lock. Nothing happened. I opened my eyes and saw the door was still intact.

What's going on? I wondered. *Maybe I'm just tired from the fight earlier.* I had used a lot of firepower. Maybe my lightning would work. It would surely wake my roommate but I didn't care. I concentrated on a lightning bolt forming at my fingertips. Sparks leaped from my fingers then quickly died. My cellmate was moving around on his bed. I was pretty sure he was about to wake up.

"What's happening?" I whispered in a panicked tone.

"It's the jumpsuit." My cellmate answered. He was looking at me but I couldn't see his face. His voice…I knew who it was. But didn't make any sense. We were in Bermuda. How did he get here? I walked over to the bunk beds and mustered up a few sparks to see my cellmate's face. The lightning was pathetic but it was just enough to see the basic details of the guy.

"X, I'd like to say I'm surprised you're here, but, at this point, I expect your randomness." I said. Although it was still dark, I could see a sly smile creep across Xavier's face.

On the other side of the prison, the female prisoners were out on the courts. A few of them were working out. Others played basketball. Sarita was off to the side, gambling with the other prisoners like she was one of them. Hannah wasn't having such a good time. She was enjoying a nice cardiovascular work out: by running for her life. Apparently, Hannah had pissed off her cellmate to the point where talking was no longer an option.

Hannah ran by the gambling girls, screaming. Sarita dropped her dice and cigarettes that she had recently won and ran to catch her friend.

"What happened?" Sarita asked as she ran beside Hannah.

"All I did was ask her which bed was mine and she said neither! So, I asked her where I was going to sleep and she said the floor. Then I said that wasn't fair and she said she hated my face!" Hannah explained to Sarita as they ran. Hannah's cellmate turned out to be a heavy smoker and she stopped chasing Hannah after less than a minute.

"You're not even worth it!" she weezed as she turned back and went to her cell.

Sarita and Hannah kept running for a while longer, just to be safe.

"I don't like prison," Hannah said to Sarita when they finally stopped running. "When are we getting out?"

"Considering the fact that we went straight from a cop car to this prison without so much as a trial, I'd say…never."

*****

"It shouldn't be taking this long!" My mom was freaking out, stateside. "Two months is more than long enough. What if something happened?"

David hugged my mom, trying to reassure her. "I'm sure they're all fine."

"How do you know?" she spat back. She was in maternal mode and my mom was convinced that I was in danger. "We have to go check."

"But they're in Bermuda! That's so far away. How would we get there?" David insisted.

My mom raised my eyebrow. "David. It's me. I know you. Don't act like you don't have some incredibly unnecessary flying invention that you wanna try out."

David smiled devilishly. "As a matter of fact, I do."

*****

That night, Danny and Chris attempted to break out of the prison. The two had been lucky enough to be cellmates.

The guards made their rounds and it was lights out. Danny waited for a few minutes then fumbled around in his pockets of his jumpsuit and pulled out a box of matches that he won in an intense game of rock, paper, scissors. He struck a match and it bathed the room in an eerie crimson glow. Chris moved in close to the bars.

"You know what to do," Danny said.

Chris nodded. He knelt to the ground and slammed his hands into the cement floors, intending to open up the ground and crush the door in the fissure. Unfortunately, neither Chris or Danny knew the effects of the jumpsuits they wore.

"What happened?" Danny asked, shocked that it didn't work.

"I'm...not sure." Chris answered, just as surprised as Danny was.

Chris tried to use his ability again. Nothing happened. Then again. Still nothing.

"I don't understand!" Chris whispered. "Danny, try yours!"

Danny tried in vain. Their powers just wouldn't work.

Danny sighed. "Dude, we're in for a long night."

I slept well that night, knowing that I had an additional friend on the inside. The next morning, X explained everything to me.

"So, these jumpsuits are inhibitors?" I asked, puzzled. At this point, I knew nothing was impossible but it was still surprising.

X quietly nodded.

"Why?" I asked then answered my own question. "This is a prison for 'special' people."

"Bingo."

"D.A.N.S.H.A.?"

"You bet."

"So, what do we do?"

X shrugged. "I can't see the future with this on." He tugged on his outfit.

"Just take it off then." I said, dumbly as if it were that easy.

"They're smart suits. Once they're on, they're on." He was right, of course. I pulled at the outfit but it squeezed tighter on my body.

"Your father's friend David designed them and D.A.N.S.H.A. stole them. They've been capturing people with abilities and holding them here for years now…" X paused as a guard walked by and peered into our cell. He pretended to be sleeping until the guard left.

"How do you get them off? Surely there's a way."

"I didn't see that far ahead. I just knew that you'd get Chris back and you'd all end up here. So, I got myself captured. All the knowledge I have now is knowledge that I gathered during the lunch sessions from older prisoners."

"Hmm. Did you get the two medallions?"

"Yes." X unzipped his mattress and the two metallic medallions shimmered lightly.

"Can you ask around to see if anyone knows how to get these things off?"

"It is worth a shot. I'll talk to my sources at the next meal." he said.

I was going to ask when that would be but I found the answer seconds later. A gruff middle aged guard shook our cell door and said, "Chow time, boys."

The cafeteria in prison was exactly as I imagined it to be: gray. The walls were off-white and made of thick bricks. There were no lights but open windows (way too high up to climb out of) near the ceiling. There were three long tables spaced evenly across the room and about ten to fifteen people sat at each one; all with the same hopeless expression on their faces. My friends all sat near each other on the middle table but they didn't seem to notice one another. Guards were everywhere, about one guard to every two prisoners. They paced the room at random intervals, looking for anything out of the ordinary.

The room was eerily quiet with the exception of slurping sounds and forks scraping trays.

I sat next to Danny. "Dude, what's going on?" I muttered, then a guard slapped his massive hairy hands on the table in front of me and growled, "Do *not* talk" then he continued pacing. Danny pretended to drink from his cup. His face was somber and devoid of emotion. He didn't even look at me when he spoke.

"We can't talk openly or the guards will come." He warned me under his breath.

He took a bite of some kind of mush that didn't look like it was ever supposed to be food and he swallowed it, painfully. I did the same and, as I pretended to chew, I told Danny that X was working on a way to get the suits off.

"That's great," Danny said through a fake yawn. The guards eyed us suspiciously and they circled the table. Across the cafeteria, X was finding out what he could about the suits when this overweight male prisoner freaked out.

"How dare you!" The heavyset man bellowed and smacked X across the face with his tray. Then he lifted X into the air and launched him across the room and he landed on my table. Xavier slid on his back until he reached me. Chris jumped from his seat and rammed the guy who had just thrown X like a rag doll, knocking the guy into two guards. Prisoner after prisoner jumped into the brawl and the guards hurried to break it up.

Danny and I stood to join in but X whispered, "No, it's a distraction. Don't worry about him. Chris is in on it." X pointed to a guard at the head of our table, near the fighting. He wore a cheap watch that looked like he bought it from a gumball machine. He was trying to pull prisoners off guards.

"That's the head guard and that watch he's wearing controls the inhibitor in our suits. Smash it and the *real* fight begins." And with that, X lunged at another prisoner who was probably in on the plan as well and started wailing on him. Guards ran to break them up and the cycle started all over again.

Fights broke out everywhere in the cafeteria and it was difficult not to be hit by a flying fist, tray or the occasional person. The head guard was more than preoccupied and he barely noticed when Danny ripped the watch off his wrist. Before he could even blink, Danny threw it on the floor and smashed it into a million pieces.

What happened next was so mind blowing! It was *the* definition of chaos. The inhibitors stopped working instantly and I have never seen more superpowers being used at once. The prisoners seemed to instinctively know that their powers were back because everyone rioted. Guards were carried into the air and dropped by flying prisoners, frozen solid by ice manipulating inmates, and jumped by copies of the same prisoner who had multiplied. The guards never stood a chance. It was indescribable mayhem and my only thought was to run. We needed to escape before reinforcements arrived.

Danny charged through the room, in the shape of a bull, knocking over anyone who got in his way. Sarita strung guard after guard from the ceiling. I had no idea where Hannah was but she was most likely invisible doing some damage...somewhere. Chris blasted stone pillars from the ground, making a rudimentary cage for the guards that had jumped on him. I shot a surge of lightning at a wall which surprised a few guards.

"We gotta go!" I screamed over the commotion and we all ran for the door. Sarita shook the handle

"We're locked in!"

"Try these!" Hannah's voice echoed from nowhere and a set of keys floated before us, she had snatched the keys from an unconscious guard.

We ran aimlessly around the prison, searching for the exit; doing away with any guard that got in the way. An alarm blared throughout the prison and more guards poured into the hallway, but it didn't matter. We were yards from the door.

"Wait!" X cried and we all froze. "I forgot the medallions!" and he darted off for our cell.

I sighed. "We can't leave him, guys." I said, hesitantly and we chased after him.

We found the cell pretty quickly and I melted the door with ease. X ripped open the mattress and snatched the medallions.

"Alright, we can go now." he stated, proudly.

"Uh, no dude, we can't." Danny corrected him. We looked back the way we came and we were trapped. Dozens of guards, with guns aimed at us, marched forward and we were cornered into my old cell.

Chris raised a wall of earth between the guards and us but we still had nowhere to run. He accidently sealed us in. It was almost pitch black except for the tiniest trickle of light from a hole in the wall behind us. The guards fired at Chris' barrier, uselessly on the other side.

"What's on the other side of this wall?" Hannah asked to no one in particular.

"Dunno but we're about to find out." I said and the room grew bright white as I charged lightning bolt and smashed a gaping hole into the wall, revealing the outside world.

The good news: we were free. The bad news: our only way out overlooked a steep cliff with jagged rocks at the bottom. It couldn't just be easy. The guards had wised up by now and were hammering away at Chris' rock wall. It was beginning to crumble and they would soon break through. We were officially out of ideas. The D.A.N.S.H.A. guards would have us in a few moments and, while we would fight as long as we could, they had us outnumbered. We would eventually be overpowered.

Outside, a faint buzzing could be heard. We didn't notice at first but it progressively got louder. After a while, it was all we could hear. The guards fired stray bullets into the cell, narrowly missing. The wall collapsed and the guards poured in but, before they could reach us, my mom and David dropped into view on an aircraft that looked like a flying inflatable raft (which was the source of the buzzing sound) and they urged us to jump in. We all piled into the craft and sped off into the sky.

The guards kept firing but we were too far away to be hit. One of the guards could be seen talking on a walkie talkie; no doubt telling his boss of our escape.

Have you ever noticed how moms always seem to know when you need them the most? Gotta love that maternal instinct!

Chapter 21

"Instruction"

Instruction: To give knowledge to; to give an order or command

to.

It had been six months since our jailbreak and we spent most of it recovering. The Phalanx had its five medallions for the Tsol Battle Championship Semi-finals so we took things easy. I gotta say, it was really nice to have a break; to do homework and not worry about some rogue aliens wanting my head on a platter.

Back at Lincoln Park, Xavier graciously thanked Dr. Bronson for all her help.

"You sure you can't stay any longer?" He asked eagerly, like a schoolboy with a crush on his teacher.

"Honestly, I don't see how much more help I could be. You have the prophecy. This is all new for me and, I'm not gonna lie, I'm a bit overwhelmed." Dr. Bronson shrugged. "But perhaps I'll visit someday." Her answer wasn't too convincing but X believed her. He waved goodbye as she pulled out of her parking spot and headed down the road.

Dr. Bronson didn't get very far before she realized she needed to fill up her tank again. The doctor pulled off to a nearby gas station and started to fuel up. She whistled a song had been stuck in her head all day while she waited. Her song was interrupted by the sound of approaching footsteps. Dr. Bronson turned to see who it was and she got a face full of chloroform.

She awoke; hours later, face down, in a dark warehouse that smelled like saw dust.

"Where am I?" she asked, groggily.

"That's none of your business, young lady." Priscilla said, taunting her.

The warehouse was dark but Dr. Bronson could see two figures, a man and a woman, standing over her.

"What...what do you want from me?"

"We want you to mind your own business. Whatever it is you think you know about the TBC, forget it. You and your little 'prophecy' are wrong." Francisco smirked.

Dr. Bronson sat up. "If I'm wrong, why do you feel the need to tell me I'm wrong? What was the point of kidnapping me?" she asked.

The couple paused then whispered something inaudible.

"You're here because you've been making a mess of our plans. And we want you to stop." Francisco explained.

"Also, we want to hear more about this prophecy." Priscilla added.

"What's in it for me if I tell you?" Dr. Bronson was stalling while she thought of a plan.

"Well, obviously we won't be letting you go anytime soon because then you'd tell Xavier and his friends about this." Priscilla reasoned.

"Obviously," Dr. Bronson agreed.

"But, if you cooperate, we'll keep the torture to a minimum. Scout's honor." Francisco gleamed.

Dr. Bronson doubted she could trust the couple as far as she could throw them but what other choice did she have?

She sighed. "What do you want to know?"

*****

Junior year had just started and even X had been enjoying the time off but all good things must come to an end. X and I were in algebra when his radar watch went off. It had been a while since he actually used the watch so he didn't realize it was his arm making the sound. Someone was calling him.

"Please turn off you cell phone, Mr. Gonzalez!" Our Prehistoric math teacher whined.

"Sorry, ma'am." he apologized while searching for his phone. It was on silent when he looked at it. Out of the corner of his eye, X noticed his watch was flashing "Call from: Mom" in yellow and "Answer Call" blinked in red below.

X flipped over his desk trying to stand up. He flew out the door without warning to answer the call, leaving the entire class stunned by his behavior.

Xavier locked himself in a stall in the boys' restroom then, when he felt the coast was clear, he pressed, "Answer Call". The watch projected a hologram of a feminine Bengal tiger with the wings of an eagle.

"Hello, Mother." X said in their native language of Seoreh.

"My dearest Drahc'ir. I am so proud of your accomplishments in reaching the semi-finals. I just wish your brother..." X's mother's voice faltered then she continued. "This isn't the call to alert you of the semi-final's location. Instead, I'm offering you advice: Train. This next year is crucial. There are forces at work that your father and I have no control over. You would do well to be cautious." she warned, still in Seoreh.

"When the time comes, I will call you again with word about the next step. Train well, my son and make me proud." The hologram began to fade and, just before it was completely gone, she added, "Oh. And your father says hi." Then she was gone.

He hadn't really thought about it, but he was in the semi-finals of the Tsol Battle Championship. The information kind of hit him all at once. He had done it: collected all five of the necessary medallions with the help of his team. It was real now. The championship was in sight. It would be so easy to just relax and leave everything to chance. But Xavier wasn't that kind of guy. *Fate favors the prepared*, he would always say.

X nodded, flushed the toilet (to keep up appearances), washed his hands, and then went back to class with a fiery determination burning in his heart.

*****

Brody was skipping school today. He felt it was warranted. He and his team had been through a lot. Not as much as the Phlanx or Legion, but still more than the average teenager goes through.

Brody sat in his room, watching a Spanish soap opera since nothing else was on during the day time hours. Carrie and Timmy were with him. I use the word "watching" loosely. Actually, no one was even looking at the screen. It was more like background noise. The three friends were lying on their backs, staring at the ceiling. They laid there silently for a while.

"Why us?" Carrie asked, breaking the silence.

"What do you mean?" Timmy asked back.

"Why were we chosen. There are like billions of people on the planet and we were chosen. Why?"

"I guess we were just lucky like that," Brody said.

"You call this *luck*? I call it a curse." Carrie spat back.

"We've got super powers!" Timmy exclaimed. "How is that not lucky?"

"Super powers with strings attached." She protested. "We *have* to fight other super human people for aliens. What do we get out of it?"

"The three rule-free wishes." Brody answered.

Carrie sat up this time. "Do you honestly think they'll give us those wishes or do you think they'll use them for themselves?"

The boys were silent.

"And even if they did give us the wishes," Carrie continued. "There are five of us and only three wishes. Who's gonna be the selfless one and give up their wish? Correction: which two people are going to be selfless and give up their wishes?"

"What do you suggest we do then, Carrie?" Timmy asked.

"We could quit." She said bluntly.

"If we quit, we go to L.I.M.B.O." Brody warned.

"Yeah, but at least we'd be in control of our lives again."

"No way!" Timmy argued. "We don't know anything about L.I.M.B.O. That's suicide!"

Their friendly conversation had escalated into a heated debate quickly.

"Frankie's dad may be somewhat shady but he's a good man. And he needs our help. Let's not forget why we agreed to do this is the first place." Brody said.

"'To help out Frankie and his friends'. Fine. I'm still in it to win it but I have one question for you." Carrie turned and looked Brody in the eyes. "What are you going to do when we have to fight Frankie and his friends in the semi-finals?"

Brody had forgotten that this was a competition and eventually our paths would cross. When that day came, only one of us would walk away from it. Would he throw the match and disappoint my father or would he send one of his best friends to L.I.M.B.O.?

Brody was speechless. It was definitely a lose-lose situation.

Timmy stepped up in Brody's silence. "We'll deal with that when the time comes. That's such a difficult decision to make. And it may not even be up to us."

Carrie paused. "I'm sorry, Brody. I didn't mean for it to sound like I was attacking you..."

"Forget about it," Brody shrugged it off. "It's kinda my fault we're in this mess anyway."

"Don't say that, dude!" Timmy protested.

"It's true though. It was my idea to skip that day. If we had been in class, like we *should've* been, this wouldn't have happened." Brody reasoned.

"Ok. No, I seriously doubt that. Don't ask me why, but I feel like this would've happened, regardless of where we were." Carrie reassured him.

"Yeah. We're in this together. No matter what." Timmy added.

Brody smiled. He was glad that his friends still had his badk.

"What do we do now, though?" Carrie wondered.

"Now?" Brody repeated the question. "Now, we wait for Mr. Lamberg to get back. If he ever gets back..."

*****

Meanwhile, back at D.A.N.S.H.A. headquarters, Francisco and Priscilla were not happy that my friends and I survived their last attack. As much as they hated to admit it, my dad was their last hope at winning the TBC and getting the three wishes. My dad had been subject to various tortures for the past 6 months as punishment for warning my friends and I about the clone assault. His body was beaten but his spirit wasn't broken.

Francisco and Priscilla summoned my dad to their throne. Two henchmen dropped him at their feet. He sat up and mustered a spiteful smile.

"Long time no see." he said and winked at them.

Priscilla fumed but Francisco calmed her down.

"You think you're clever, Lamberg. However, we disagree. Our patience has worn thin with you but we're giving you an opportunity to redeem yourself. Your team has collected the five medallions necessary to compete in the TBC semi-finals. We are releasing you to train your squad for it. Do *not* disappoint us again or we will make good on our promise to ruin your life."

Francisco snapped his fingers and had my dad was escorted away. Priscilla leaned over to Francisco. "Can we really trust him to do what we need him to do?" she whispered.

He laughed. "That's unclear. And I'm skeptical regardless. But do not worry, my love. Now that we have the prophecy in our possession, we'll be unstoppable. I've seen this scenario in many different ways. And they all end well for us."

"What about the billions of people dying? I'm all for murder but that's a bit excessive." Priscilla said, uneasily.

"Not to worry. That won't happen. I've seen all the outcomes and that's not one of them."

"But what if something changes?" Priscilla continued, persistently.

"Then we're covered. I have a safeguard up my sleeve."

Priscilla was confused. "A safeguard? What safeguard?"

Francisco held Priscilla's hand tenderly. "Patience, dear. Good things come to those who wait."

Chapter 22

"Preparation"

Preparation: To make ready beforehand for some purpose, use,

or activity.

Another month had passed since X got the call from home and everyone was preparing for something. My dad and his team were training for the TBC. The phalanx was doing the same. D.A.N.S.H.A. was getting ready to release their "safeguard". But, personally, I was excited for my 17th birthday that was a day away. The conditions of this birthday would surely be better than last year. The Phalanx was back and better than ever, my dad was alive, I learned a bit about the history of my parents and we were in the semi-finals of the TBC. Sure, there were bad things to focus on; like the fact that Laura was still gone and the Legion as well but there was no need to dwell on that because it couldn't be changed. Or, at least, that's what I thought.

In L.I.M.B.O., the Legion had a choice to make. Stay in a virtual utopia or return to reality and help their friends. They each thought about who they left behind. Curt thought about Hannah. He knew he needed to make amends and protect her from harm. Jared considered the options but had made up his mind a while ago to never lose to me in any competition again. Staci needed to restore her honor and credibility for having fallen for such a simple trick. Jayden wanted to prove her worth and prowess of her ability. Derrick thought about his brother,

Xavier. Facing his inner demons in L.I.M.B.O. had given him a new outlook on life and Derrick had to beg his brother's forgiveness. Everyone had a reason to return to reality so the answer was obvious.

"Sir," Staci started, respectfully. "We've all got people waiting for us and, as amazing as staying here would be, we have some business to take care of."

The hologram of David smiled. "Excellent choice. You have passed your third and final test in L.I.M.B.O. You have all earned your freedom."

Everything went white and the five friends woke up suspended in pods full of liquid. The fluid drained out of the pods and their doors opened. The Legion stepped out of the pods and quickly fell to the ground. Months of inactivity had made their muscles weak but thanks to one of David's many inventions, they had full control of their bodies in no time. Dahlia and John helped the Legion get their balance, and then led them to David.

"Well done," he applauded when he saw the teens. "You have amazing timing. Frankie and his friends are in danger. I have no idea how they did it but D.A.N.S.H.A..." Curt raised his hand as if he were in class. "Yes, Curtis?"

"What's D.A.N.S.H.A.?"

"Ah. Yes. Forgive me. I forgot you all are a bit behind on the times." He then proceeded to explain that they had been in L.I.M.B.O. for about a year and updated them on the essentials.

"As I was saying," David continued after getting the Legion up to speed. "D.A.N.S.H.A. has somehow redirected a secondary meteor shower to attack San Antonio; Lincoln High School to be exact, in a last ditch effort to knock them out of the TBC. Tomorrow morning, I need you six to warn them and help them out in anyway you can..." Curt raised his hand again.

David was getting annoyed. "*Yes*, Curt?"

"You said six. There are only five of us."

"That's where you're wrong," David smiled. "Come on in!" He called into the hall and a 5'5 blonde girl with a tiny frame came into the room. She had a soft, oval face and light brown eyes. She smiled brightly when she saw the Legion. Everyone's jaw was on the floor. Curt stuttered dumbly as he tried to process the information. All he could manage to say was a name.

"Laura…"

I awoke the next morning, bright and early. It was my 17th birthday and I couldn't be more excited. The shower ran perfectly and when I got out, there was a note on the bed, similar to last year. Another promise to go out to dinner; just my mom, David, and me. Now that I think about it, I never cashed in on the first dinner. *I'll have to fix that*, I thought. I dressed quickly and headed to the bus stop.

I stood at the bus stop with a huge smile on my face until one of my classmates innocently asked, "Where's Derrick?"

I froze. All evil deeds aside, I missed the guy.

"I dunno," I answered, honestly. It was the truth. But, somehow I knew, wherever he was, Derrick was fine.

The bus was late but nothing could dampen my spirits. I was walking on sunshine. I found my usual seat and said hi to X, Danny, Sarita, and Hannah; who all wished me happy birthday as the bus jerked to a start and drove us to school.

The bus ride was uneventful and we were at school before we knew it. Chris met us under the arch of the school and we were about to go to class when a golf ball sized rock smashed into the cement in front of us. Puzzled, we looked to the sky and realized that it wasn't a rock at all; it was a meteorite. One of thousands, actually; The sky was littered with them. There were some the size of baseballs, others the size of basketballs and a few as big as sedans. And they were all heading for one place: Lincoln High School.

I looked at my friends and we all exchanged a mutual "Oh, Crap" look. Meteorite pieces would rain down on the school in moments and, if we didn't act fast, our school would be destroyed.

Preparation

We would've just let it happen but the school was full of roughly 3,000 unsuspecting high school students. My friends and I knew we were the only ones that could save the school and it was our job to figure out exactly how to do that. And they said there was nothing special about turning 17…

Here's a Sneak Peek at the third
and final book in the Star Struck
Trilogy:

STAR STRUCK
CULMNATION

The Prologue

It's all over. We did the best we could but D.A.N.S.H.A. won the Tsol Battle Championship and, with one of their wishes, they inadvertently killed 90% of the human population. My friends and I are lucky to be alive. The bad guys have won. Morale is really low. But we can't give up. D.A.N.S.H.A. still has a wish or two left and they have to be stopped. As pathetic as it sounds, the fate of mankind rests in the hands of high school kids. No pressure, right?

If you're wondering how it got this bad, it's a very complicated story. One that involves flashbacks, time traveling, and a third meteor shower. The only thing I ask is that you try your best not to get lost. Where to start...well, I guess the second meteor shower is as good a place as any. By the way, have you ever tried to stop a meteor shower? Let me tell you, it is not fun...

www.ingramcontent.com/pod-product-compliance
Lightning Source LLC
Chambersburg PA
CBHW031845170626
46807CB00004B/1624